WENSLEY CLARKSON was one of Britain's most successful young journalists before leaving London for Los Angeles with his wife and four children in 1991 – an experience which inspired his book, *A Year In La La Land*. His other books include the tabloid newspaper exposé, *Dog Eat Dog*, as well as four best-selling British true crime books including *Hell Hath No Fury* and *Love You To Death, Darling*. He has written biographies of actors Mel Gibson and Tom Cruise and his extraordinary true crime book, entitled *Whatever Mother Says*, is due for publication in Britain and the U.S. in the summer of 1995. He currently divides his time between homes in London and California. *An Eye For An Eye* is his twelfth book.

AN
EYE
FOR
AN
EYE

# AN
# EYE
# FOR
# AN
# EYE

Wensley Clarkson

**BLAKE**

Published by Blake Publishing Ltd,
3 Bramber Court, 2 Bramber Road, London W14 9PB, England

First published in Great Britain in 1995

ISBN 1 85782 116 5

British Library Cataloguing-in-Publication Data:
A catalogue record for this book is available from
the British Library.

Typeset by Pearl Graphics, Hemel Hempstead

Printed in Finland by WSOY

1 3 5 7 9 10 8 6 4 2

To Clare . . . for not avenging me

# CONTENTS

# NOTES OF GRATITUDE

The idea of using a leaden, dispassionate word like 'acknowledgements' for this section cannot begin to express the depth of my feelings for the many individuals who have made this book possible. I owe them my deepest and most heartfelt gratitude.

First, to my publisher John Blake, without whom this book would never have happened. His support and guidance have been very much appreciated.

Then there is forensic psychiatrist Dr Peter Wood who not only provided me with an expert's introduction to this intriguing subject but also patiently revealed to me a unique insight into women and revenge.

Numerous criminologists, journalists and families of the

subjects themselves provided invaluable assistance – some from as far away as California and Norway.

Last, but by no means least there are: John Glatt, Mark Sandelson, Graeme Gourlay, Martin Dunn, John Bell, Peter Wilson, Joe Poalella, Sadie Mayne, Rosie Ries and every other person who agreed to help with the research for this book. Also, my eternal thanks to the reference libraries at News International, London and *The Daily News* in New York, as well as to *The Sunday Times*, *Daily Telegraph*, *Daily Mirror*, *The Sun*, *The Evening Standard* and all the other sources of reference material which has proved so inspirational for this book.

# FOREWORD

*Dr Peter Wood, forensic psychiatrist, who has investigated four hundred killings.*

As a forensic psychiatrist who has investigated more than four hundred cases of murder, I would say that everyone has the capacity to seek revenge.

However, women seem to break the law more frequently for reasons of revenge, although when it comes actually to murdering someone they often involve more than one other person. Women who set out to gain revenge seem to go completely over the top.

Men often become their token victims. Frequently, these women have been abused during their childhood and are looking for a male victim.

In recent years I have also noticed that violent behaviour in young women is increasing faster than it is in young men. Yet, intriguingly, more than half of the women serving life for murder didn't strike the final blow themselves. I put this fact down to the manipulative skills of women who, although it may seem sexist of me to say so, seem capable of persuading others to do their dirty work for them. I've dealt with numerous cases where women have been convicted of conspiracy or of trying to recruit a hired killer. It is almost as if they find it easier to keep themselves one step removed from the actual crimes they wish to commit.

I get called into a case either by the prosecution or the defence. I work wholly independently. I have found the most difficult criminal cases to solve to be the ones where somebody has done something inexplicable and where they seem totally ordinary – an apparently motiveless crime.

In psychiatric terms, I usually look at three or four aspects of a case and it is imperative that I start with virtually no knowledge of the offence that has been committed. I might have a headline from a newspaper, but nothing more than that when I go to see someone for the first time. They have to tell me themselves what they have done.

I then start collecting information from other sources – the more the better – from relatives, medical notes, school reports, comments from employers, even witnesses' statements. I also examine the notes that the police collect about a defendant's background. If someone has a psychiatric history, I would read their psychiatric notes or GP's notes. I then see the subject several times in the course of a remand period.

Many of the crimes described in *An Eye For An Eye* are either partly or wholly caused by a clearly defined inequality of the sexes. In these modern times the woman is often the more successful breadwinner while the man is more and more likely to be a dead loss. Women get angry about this because they so often still end up running the home single-handed. It is almost as if their position in life has become even more stressful, instead of more equal.

Undoubtedly, the biggest difference between men and women is that women don't seem to need to beat their chests and show how tough and strong they are. They can still usually just walk away from an over-sensitive, brittle male who continues to say 'no' at his peril. But when women do decide they have had enough, it behoves men everywhere to beware...

Dr Peter J. W. Wood,
M.B. B.S. (LOND), M.R.C.S., L.R.C.P., D.P.M., M.R.C. Psych.
Consultant Forensic Psychiatrist,
Bradford, Yorkshire,
February 1995

'Vengeance is a specific virtue.'

Thomas Aquinas, *Summa Theologica*

'Revenge is a kind of wild justice,
which the more man's nature runs to,
the more ought law to weed it out.'

Francis Bacon

'Revenge is never a good word to use
because it can affect innocent people.'

Margaret Thatcher

# PROLOGUE

'Revenge', says the well-known proverb, 'is a dish best served cold.' There are a couple of ways to look at that, but you could also take the advice of the hotheaded Roman who penned, 'Hammer your iron when it's glowing hot.'

Regardless of temperature, revenge is an ancient human motive; and, as the media frenzy over *l'affaire* Bobbitt shows, it remains as compelling as ever. The revenge-starved beast resides within all of us and the idea that a random change in fortune – heartbreak or disappointment perhaps – might unleash the monster arouses a universal feeling of dread.

A new breed of villain is emerging. Evoking fear, outrage and incomprehension in equal proportions, the so-called 'new female criminal' has been identified as a species unique to our time. Home Office figures show that in the past decade violent crimes by women went up by 67 per cent, compared with 10 per cent among men. The leap since 1973 has been 250 per cent, and in America the rise during the eighties was 62 per cent.

However, men are not always to blame. Some, as in many of the cases highlighted in this book, fell victim to unprovoked violence from the women they love.

Revenge is one of the most natural and understandable of human emotions. Which of us, on the losing end of an argument, has not felt the twinge of an urge to get even? Take the instance of the lady who, having been jilted by her lover, used his telephone to ring the speaking clock long-distance when he was away for the weekend, leaving him with a rather hefty bill. All rather amusing and harmless.

We become more torn, however, when we hear about the sort of cases highlighted in *An Eye For An Eye*. Instinct tells us that we would never commit crimes in the name of revenge, but is that really the case? One cannot help feeling sympathy for people who genuinely believe the law has let them down.

We think of our loved ones and how we might react if they were molested or even killed by some unthinking brute who is then treated with undue leniency by the courts. Taking the law into one's own hands in such circumstances is suddenly not unthinkable. It is understandable, if not excusable.

The entire question of guilt when such cases come to court is, of course, a matter for a judge and jury. If they convict, though, what does the judge do when the person he or she is about to sentence has taken the law into their own hands? The sentence must recognise the fact that the law cannot condone private vendettas and vengeance. The reasonable onlookers of whom the law speaks are known to have sympathy and compassion, however, and the sentence can perfectly properly reflect the fact.

A female out to get her own back is always going to be a dangerous animal. Revenge is fast becoming a traditionally female art because vengeful women are deadlier than men. They are also much cleverer.

Women with broken hearts seem more determined to seek their revenge or even launch a murderous scheme. The way these females see it, they are the victims and it is only fair to pass on some of that pain to whoever inflicted it in the first place.

Women don't always get it right. Sometimes their victims end up being heralded as heroes for standing up to their vengeful partners. However, in the back of every other female's mind is the thought that they can understand why that crime was committed.

There are other ominous signs in today's society that women who perpetrate violent acts are being wrongly let off.

At a recent London conference on adolescent and female offenders given by the International Association for Forensic Psychotherapists, Dr Estella Weldon issued a warning that as long as we continue to reinforce the image of women as victims and men as perpetrators, society will remain blind to female offenders.

More women are now seeking revenge because of poverty, homelessness, single parenthood, dependency on drugs and alcohol, or to escape an intolerable family environment. In short, to survive, which isn't so different from what men do.

There has never been any real evidence that women are inherently any less destructive, aggressive or dangerous than men. So why is it that each time a violent woman strikes, reason is hijacked by primitive emotion? Women's crimes are still guaranteed to touch a raw nerve in ways unequalled by those of even the most monstrous of male psychopaths.

It is also time to recognise that there can be a positive side to female aggression, as there always was. To deny the female 'shadow' is to diminish women as human beings and to ignore how often history has disproved the myth of women's passivity. Whether we like it or not, the female shadow has become a force to be reckoned with.

# 1

'Behaviour that is labelled violent or
sexual in a man is usually considered
benign in a woman.'

Heidi Vanderbilt

# NO REGRETS

Striking, willowy Elaine had never believed in love at first sight – until she found herself sitting opposite an elegant, distinguished-looking, council-housing boss named Michael. Elaine was just twenty-six years old but, with two young children to support single-handed, she was facing an uphill task and the noisy neighbours in the block of cramped flats where she lived were the last straw.

She hoped the visit to her local council-housing offices would result in a transfer to a better home. However, as she sat there opposite the handsome housing official in his elegant, pale grey suit, her mind started to wander a million miles from the everyday problems she was facing.

Elaine certainly cut a fine figure compared with most

of the applicants for housing transfers who turned up to see Michael Friend. Elaine tended to favour pencil-slim black mini-skirts with dark stockings and patent three-inch stilettos to show off her good legs.

As she sat in that neat, tidy office in September 1990, Michael could not help noticing Elaine's well-proportioned legs and fashionable hairstyle. She hardly looked like a desperately poor, virtually on-the-breadline council tenant but then Elaine was always one for keeping up appearances. She loved to be admired by men in a healthy sort of way. She knew that she had 'it', because she was forever getting admiring glances in the street. She also had a quietly confident air about her. Elaine was never over-awed. She always believed it was important to look good, however many problems might lie beneath the surface.

She could see something in Michael's attitude towards her which sparked an instant chemistry, perhaps even a feeling of romance. She also recognised that he was, outwardly, a fine, upstanding citizen with a highly responsible, well-paid job, while she was one of his 'clients'.

Every now and again Elaine would alter her sitting position on the chair opposite his desk, unconsciously giving Michael a new angle on her shapely legs. He responded awkwardly; unable to resist glancing at them but touchingly diffident about letting her know the fact that he was utterly swamped with desire.

Elaine noticed the glances from Michael and smiled back gently. Occasionally, their eyes would actually meet and Michael would look away shyly. He sensed that something was happening. As Elaine explained what life was like living in the tiny flat following her divorce, Michael's mind kept wandering back to those legs, that face, the curvaceous body.

Elaine told Michael how she struggled up and down fourteen steps each and every time she took baby daughter Francesca and toddler James out of the flat.

'I am not expecting to be treated as a special case,' said Elaine, once again shifting her position and unconsciously giving Michael yet another glance at her black nylons. 'I just want to know how long it is going to take to get a transfer.'

Michael nodded his head sympathetically. He said he perfectly understood her dilemma and he did not blame her for coming right to the top for a solution. It was then that Elaine realised that the words he was speaking bore no relation to the thoughts going through his mind.

'It was as if there was an unspoken subtext,' she later recalled. And Elaine was right because forty-eight-year-old Michael was gradually sinking in a sea of love. The young mother sitting opposite him seemed one of the most beautiful women he had ever met.

Snapping himself back to the subject at hand, Michael tried to sound caring. It simply had the effect of drawing the two of them even closer together.

Michael said he knew exactly what it must be like for Elaine to live under such dire conditions. She was pleasantly surprised to hear this kind of response from a council official as she was more used to negative replies and meaningless sympathy.

'I know what it is like not to own a home of your own,' Michael said quietly but with great purpose. This time it was Elaine's turn to feel awkward. For the first time she knew that he was starting to change the course of their conversation.

Then Michael admitted that he had been living in a rented bungalow after his own marriage had broken up. Elaine suddenly realised that the entire purpose of her visit to those offices had switched direction. Soon Michael was doing most of the talking, even telling Elaine that he had a grandson of a similar age to her own son. Ten minutes after walking into a stranger's office to plead for better accommodation, Elaine was feeling romantic rapport with a man old enough to be her father.

However, it has to be said that, throughout their first meeting, Michael never actually flirted or behaved in any way improperly towards his 'client'. On the surface, he was entirely professional in his approach, although he undoubtedly did not always talk about his own personal problems with every council tenant with an axe to grind.

As Elaine got up to leave Michael's office, she could feel a rush of passion travelling through her body. She felt it as she lingered while she shook his hand, making it last a few seconds longer than normal. She then caught his eyes one last time and he looked down uneasily. She also knew that as she walked out of that office on those three-inch heels, he was watching the contours of her body. She could not resist a little swagger as she departed.

Later that same day, Elaine's telephone rang just as she walked in from an exhausting afternoon with the children.

'Hello, this is Michael Friend. Look at your watch,' he said. Elaine hesitated for a moment, then remembered him from the meeting that morning. However, it was a fairly unconventional way to start a phone conversation and she was bemused. She looked at her watch and it was 5.32 p.m.

'This is my own time and I'm ringing to ask you out for a drink tomorrow night.'

Typically, Michael had responded to the chance of a romance in a perfectly upstanding, thoroughly legitimate way. He had thought about Elaine virtually every minute of the day from the moment she had walked out of his office that morning. He'd counted the minutes and hours until he was 'off duty'. Michael knew that it would have been improper to ask a council tenant for a date until he was officially finished for the day. Now, just two short minutes after his self-imposed deadline, he was nervously asking the object of his desire to come out for a drink.

Elaine was completely unsurprised by the call from Michael, although she was somewhat apprehensive about the fact that she was about to allow herself to get embroiled with a man who was old enough to be her father. That slight reluctance was tempered, and ultimately outbalanced, by the flattery she felt because a man with such a powerful, well-paid job was obviously interested in her.

Within seconds of hearing his slightly hesitant voice on the other end of the line, Elaine began to take control of the situation. She also could not help feeling a tingle of excitement at the prospect of starting a relationship with a man of such high social standing in the community.

Elaine always felt somewhat disappointed that her own relationships had failed because she had come from such a loving and close-knit family. She also felt slightly embarrassed to be living in such poor accommodation because her own upbringing had been rather privileged. Her father had been a company director and he had always made sure Elaine got exactly what she wanted. There were two ponies which provided the perfect diversion for the young, teenage Elaine who grew to love the thrill of riding in the country much more than the idea of parties or nightclubs.

That love of horses had even provided Elaine with the perfect job as a groom in the United States when she was in her late teens. However, all through her teenage years and early twenties, Elaine had suffered from the problems that are often associated with being a volatile, impulsive – and very attractive – young woman. Her love of passion and sex were unquestionable and she hoped that, in a perfect world, those two magic ingredients would combine to provide her with the perfect marriage.

Unfortunately, Elaine's first marriage had started with a flurry of love making, followed by two children in fast succession and then a lot of arguments and unhappiness, caused primarily by the sort of problems that beset so many young, recently wed couples.

That was why an older, more responsible man like Michael Friend seemed to hold the key to Elaine's happiness. She believed that he would not only offer her security but a chance to redeem herself following a string of passionate, yet disaster-prone, relationships.

The couple's first date the following evening simply confirmed those prospects for Elaine. She had spent much of the afternoon deliberating about what to wear for that first taste of romance. Her dilemma was that she did not want to look like some floozy on the arm of an elder man. Nor did she want to end up looking old before her time. However, she need not have worried. Elaine was the sort of woman who always ended up looking good.

Eventually, she decided to play it very conservatively by wearing a soft, brown leather jacket and smart, tailored trousers. It was a good choice in the circumstances because Michael Friend was not a man to be rushed into anything, or so it seemed.

That first date at a pleasant, cosy pub in old Portsmouth, Hampshire, went with ease. It was almost as if the couple had known each other for years. Michael needed someone to tell about his entire life and Elaine was more than happy to listen as he talked about his passion for golf and hockey and his two previous marriages.

Elaine even surprised herself by not batting an eyelid when he told her about his son at university and his daughter who was married with a little boy. Instead of worrying about the age difference between them, Elaine started to warm towards him even more. She was intrigued by the idea of a romance with an older man. She wondered if an older man's experience would rub off in every sense of the word.

At the end of that first meeting, Michael ingratiated himself further with Elaine by acting like the perfect gentle-man. He drove her home in his gleaming Mercedes and did not even press her to let him into the flat. In fact, she had to insist on him coming in for coffee. After drinking a cup, he asked her out for dinner the next night. He left the flat with nothing more than an awkward kiss on the cheek.

That night Elaine found herself consumed with thoughts about this new, older man in her life. She was used to throwing herself into a relationship but here was a man who wanted to take his time. Maybe this was the one who would actually lead to eternal happiness?

The following evening the chemistry between them continued to work. The more they both poured out to each other details about their backgrounds, the more they felt locked together. The overriding emotion for Elaine was flattery. Here was a warm, sensitive, intelligent man who obviously respected her. She listened avidly as he regaled her with stories about his own wealthy antique dealer father; how his mother had tragically died giving birth to him; how he had been packed off to boarding school at the age of six.

Elaine soaked up his background. She wanted to peel away as many layers of his life as possible so that she could get to grips with what made him tick. She would counter his stories with recollections about her own family. The more they revealed to each other, the warmer the inner emotions became. It was the sort of love game many new couples enjoy. The disclosure of personal details bonds people much closer together.

What impressed Elaine most was that Michael never once spoke down to her. Not once was he patronising or condescending. In fact, he made it clear that he considered himself to be incredibly lucky to have her. It was the sort of courtship that women the world over dream of enjoying.

Michael did not hesitate to ask Elaine to bring along her two young children when they went out on their fourth date just three days later. He happily welcomed the youngsters into his rented bungalow and did not mind about the mess they caused. In fact, it was Michael who suggested they enjoy a family day out in the nearby New Forest.

There was a hidden motive for that trip. Elaine was surprised but delighted when Michael asked her to marry him even although it was just four days since they had first met. Little Francesca was asleep in the back of the car and Elaine could not quite believe her ears at first. His request for her hand in marriage made her feel so good. It was just so amazing for her to find herself the object of such genuine romantic interest. Instead of rushing her into the nearest bed, Michael had wooed and coaxed her and provided her with a feeling of security. There was only one possible reply to his question: 'Yes'.

As they drove home, snatching each other's hands at every opportunity, Elaine kept thinking to herself: *'At last my life is going somewhere. At last my life is going somewhere.'*

.   .   .

The wedding was as white and romantic as anything could be for two divorcees in a register office. Just a handful of friends and relatives were present. Elaine's mother had tears in her eyes as she watched the happy couple kiss for the first time as husband and wife.

Unfortunately, Elaine's father did not feel similarly impressed. He refused to attend the marriage because he deeply disapproved of his daughter marrying a man the same age as himself. Even more ominously, he also predicted that the relationship would end in tears. Elaine, swept along by a tide of romance and passion, passed off her father's attitude as typical of a father's concern for his daughter. She was confident that he would eventually come around to liking Michael and accept him as a son-in-law.

Michael Friend seemed to have no blemishes whatsoever.

Elaine believed he had risked his entire career by marrying her. Meanwhile, the gossips of the housing department had a field day when word got around that quietly-spoken Michael was marrying a council tenant whom he had first met when she went to his office. As word filtered through the building that she had a penchant for black stockings, high heels and mini-skirts, it simply fuelled the blaze of innuendo.

Elaine was well aware of all this and it simply made her feel even more in love with Michael. To think he had taken such a huge risk by marrying her simply proved what a fine man he was.

When Michael was promoted to chief executive six months later and rewarded with a hefty salary increase, it made Elaine feel even more thrilled because it seemed to be a confirmation of Michael's colleagues' acceptance of their relationship.

Elaine was also pleased by Michael's off-duty attitude. Despite the age difference, he was proving an imaginative, energetic lover. Elaine found it quite a turn-on going to bed with this older man. He was so much more patient and caring than her previous lovers.

For the first year of marriage, the age-factor never even reared its head. Elaine and Michael both enjoyed love making and she felt more sexually satisfied than at any other time in her life.

The only slight disappointment for Elaine was that Michael remained as quiet in bed as he was during their waking hours. While Elaine enjoyed a certain level of passionate bed-talk, he was definitely the strong, silent type. However, it wasn't the end of the world for Elaine. She relished her new role as a civic wife, attending important council functions at the Town Hall.

Michael was clearly besotted with his young wife and she would frequently catch him glancing at her lovingly across busy, crowded receptions. It was a look of passion that she treasured.

Michael did not hesitate to lavish gifts on Elaine: beautiful clothes, a watch to match his own, a pricy sports car. In fact, Michael's only weakness in terms of himself seemed to be his love of Mercedes cars. He was like a child in a sweet shop when he took Elaine to a nearby showroom to choose a new £27,000 red Mercedes 230E to replace his older model. Michael admired the bodywork as if it was a piece of art and when they drove it home together, Elaine felt a rush of passion the moment her legs touched the lush leather seats.

However, the ultimate gift from Michael to Elaine was the house. Within a year of their marriage, Michael had bought a dream home for his new young family – a beautiful Georgian property in a select area of Alverstoke in Hampshire. It was a truly magnificent family home, something that Elaine had coveted all her adult life. She became so consumed with the house and making sure the furnishings and decorations were just perfect that she did not at first notice how much more withdrawn Michael was becoming.

Initially, she presumed it was because he was preoccupied with work; that it was a passing phase and that he would soon relax. Instead, Michael started to withdraw even more into his shell. Elaine was reluctant to face the fact that there might be problems. She knew that Michael had taken on a vast mortgage to pay for the house but surely such a responsible, caring, cautious man would never allow himself to become over-committed?

Michael was slipping rapidly into a state of virtual non-communication. The couple spent many evenings barely uttering a word to each other and, when they did, he tended to sound as if he was addressing a council meeting. Elaine would say something highly inane, like: 'Aren't there a lot of people about?' just to break the deathly silence that filled their lovely home. But then Michael would reply, 'Yes, this road does carry a lot of pedestrians.'

Elaine did not need a master's degree in psychology to know that something was wrong, yet her frustration was caused by the fact that he did not talk about it or get angry or even cry. She was used to tempestuous relationships where, if there was a problem, it would be brought out into the open.

Here, however, was a remote, unhappy man offering no anger, no recrimination, no argument, just stony silence. The end result of this complete inability to communicate was that Elaine started to feel extremely lonely. She craved a hug and cuddle in bed each night, just as a sign of reassurance, but none was forthcoming.

Whenever Elaine tried to snuggle up alongside her husband, she was greeted with a complete lack of response. Sometimes she would try to surprise him when he came home with a candle-lit supper, a glance of stocking top, some shiny silk underwear, but Michael did not acknowledge a thing. He was either so depressed by his life that he did not feel any sexual urge or he had found someone else.

One night Elaine found herself lying wide awake going

over the problems of her marriage, wondering where she had gone wrong, why everything had fallen apart. Next to her, Michael did not utter a word. She knew he was awake but she simply did not know what to talk to him about. She knew that if she stroked or kissed him, he would simply go rigid and pretend to be asleep.

Finally, she spoke. 'What are you thinking about?'

'Nothing.'

His reply sounded weak and frail. She felt an over-whelming urge to comfort him. She snuggled up to him.

'I thought beds were for sleeping in,' Michael said in a cold voice.

Elaine stopped dead. The man who had made such warm, passionate caring love to her until just a few months earlier had become this stranger beside her. She felt completely and utterly rejected and hurt. There was a deep silence between them, broken only by the occasional car headlights flashing by outside.

Elaine waited maybe a minute longer in the hope that he might say, 'Sorry', but he did not. She got out of the bed and walked into the spare bedroom next door. After just fifteen months together, the marriage seemed to be over.

In the back of her mind, Elaine wondered if it was the financial pressures that were getting to him. The gifts – a smart car, two horses, expensive perfume – were constant reminders. Perhaps he had bought them for her to appease her and silence her like a father with a nagging, talkative child?

In the months following Elaine's decision to sleep in a separate bed, the atmosphere worsened. She took to walking the dog just to escape the long awkward silences that had become part of her home life whenever Michael was around. Things got so bad that he avoided all conversation by giving her one-syllable replies to all her questions. The only time they ever talked about anything it tended to be riveting subjects like the weather and what was on the television that evening.

Worst of all, Michael had gone from being an energetic, passionate man of forty-eight to an old man of fifty. In July of that year, the inevitable happened and Michael moved out. This was when the marriage went into a strange reverse gear.

.   .   .

Within a few weeks, Elaine rediscovered sex and passion from the most unlikely of sources – her estranged husband. Having moved out of the matrimonial home, Michael began to pop back to see her and the children and, some would say inevitably, the couple ended up in bed together.

For the first time in months the sex between them was entirely compatible and highly enjoyable. They started to do things to each other that they had never even tried before. Elaine was in a state of total confusion. On the one hand, she had a healthy appetite for love making and he was satisfying that urge, but once they had completed the act he would calmly get dressed and bid her farewell before setting off for his new bachelor pad in the gleaming red Mercedes.

After one particularly energetic sex session, Elaine pleaded with him to move back into the house and try to repair their broken marriage. Even though, minutes earlier, they had been locked in passion, Michael refused.

Elaine cried that night. She was bemused, upset and

angry. She felt used in some ways. but kept clinging to the hope that their love making was a sign that one day he would come back. She just could not work out why he refused to move back into the family home. She became extremely obsessive about Michael and started to wonder what was happening in his other life, when he was not in her bed making love to her.

She took to driving past his rented house every so often. She wanted to know what he did when he was not with her. One night she recognised the car of one of Michael's female colleagues parked outside his home. The penny dropped instantly and she concluded, rightly or wrongly, that he was having an affair with this woman.

Elaine thought back to all the times when she had seen her husband chatting to this woman. She recalled occasions when she had been entering Michael's office just as the other woman was coming out. Images began flashing through her mind. She remembered their closeness, the fleeting glances. She had also never forgotten that once she had even confronted him about the woman and he had insisted they were 'just friends', although he had confessed that he and this lady had been lovers some years previously.

All the pieces of the jigsaw seemed to fit together with frightening ease. Elaine believed they must still be lovers and she convinced herself that this woman was the one her husband had wanted all along. She hated herself for letting him come back into her bed because she felt lonely. She hated herself for initiating such pleasurable sex. She hated herself for being such a fool.

Elaine's pride was crushed. She concluded that Michael

would not recommit himself to her because he wanted this other woman. She confronted him the next time he came round for sex. He insisted there was no relationship and seemed genuinely upset that his estranged wife should think otherwise.

For a few moments Elaine thought that perhaps she was leaping to the wrong conclusion. In any case, here he was in their home. He even offered her a shoulder to cry on when she become increasingly distraught. She weakened that night and let him make love to her again but it wasn't as good as it had been because she kept thinking about that other woman and she wondered if Michael was also picturing her as they explored each other.

A few weeks later, Elaine even confronted the woman herself when she visited Michael at his office. Just like Michael, she insisted they were just friends but Elaine could not help noticing how protective she was about Michael.

Elaine had reached rock bottom. Her confrontations meant that Michael did not come round so often to make love to her. Her obsession with trying to save her marriage became more twisted and out of control. Often she would drive past the other woman's house to check whether Michael's red Mercedes was parked outside. This went on for months. She never actually caught him out but her obsession continued to grow at an alarming rate.

One day, a stack of post addressed to Michael arrived at Elaine's house. Usually she would drop it off at his home but on this occasion it was too bulky to go through the letter box. Elaine rang Michael's home number and left a message on the answering machine but he never bothered to reply.

Elaine was infuriated by her estranged husband's off-hand attitude. He expected to be able to call round at her home for love-making sessions but he would not even take the time out to call her back. Elaine began to feel great waves of anger and tension. Her head was throbbing. She felt used, abused, ill-treated. She tried to watch TV that night but her mind kept going back to him. He was the cause of all her anxiety. He was the one who came round for sex and then discarded her like some secret mistress.

By midnight, Elaine could stand it no longer. She stormed out of the house and drove round to Michael's home. His car wasn't there. She presumed he must have been with *her*. That made things even worse.

Elaine dumped the mail on his porch and then stormed round to her rival's house. On the way, she found it difficult even to concentrate on her driving. The street lights became a blur and she jumped traffic lights because nothing had any significance other than finding out if Michael was there.

When she got to the other woman's house her heart sank. Michael's immaculate red Mercedes was parked outside. She did not know whether to cry or shriek with satisfaction. One side of her wanted to trap him while the other was hoping that none of it was true.

She glanced up from the car to the house and saw that an upstairs light was on. She killed the engine and sat in silence for a few moments before taking a deep breath. Then she got out of the car quietly and walked up the pathway. From the upstairs room she had definitely heard laughing. She stopped to listen intently. It was so quiet she could hear her own breathing and feel her heart thumping.

She waited for what seemed like minutes, but was probably only twenty or thirty seconds, before she heard his voice and then *hers*. Elaine could barely make out what was being said, then she heard an unmistakable name being mentioned, *'Elaine'*. They were talking about her, laughing about her behind her back.

Right then Elaine snapped back to reality. What the hell was she doing crouching like some peeping Tom outside a house where her husband was with another woman?

*'Forget it, Elaine. Forget it,'* she kept saying to herself over and over again. It was ludicrous. She should just walk away and never see him again. But the other side of Elaine was eaten with rage. Here was the man who continued to expect to make love to her, who had dumped her in a lifestyle she couldn't possibly afford and left her stranded in a house that neither of them could ever maintain.

She thought about shouting up at them and confronting them but that seemed too easy a solution. She suspected they would only laugh in her face anyhow. It would have damaged her pride and her self-respect. No, there had to be a better way to get revenge on that two-timing husband. There had to be a way to hit him where it really hurt.

Elaine felt inside her handbag for the spare key to her husband's beautiful new Mercedes. She had already decided that she was going to send a very special message to him. She moved silently and swiftly across the front garden of the house towards the car. She unlocked it, got into the driving seat and switched on the ignition. It started first time. She carefully reversed out of the drive, wondering if he would hear what was happening and rush out, but nothing happened. Perhaps the illicit lovers were so consumed with passion that they were oblivious to what was happening just a few feet away.

As Elaine headed towards town in her husband's pride and joy she felt a surge of excitement. But what was she going to do with the car? How could she use it to hurt that cheating man? For a few moments she even considered turning around. It wasn't too late and Michael would probably never be the wiser. After all, she felt a certain attachment to the car as she had helped him to choose it. Maybe she should let sleeping dogs lie?

Then something strange happened to Elaine. She found herself taking the fastest route to the Town Hall where her husband and his girlfriend worked. To this day, Elaine says she does not know what inspired her to go there. She insists it was a subconscious reaction.

It was twelve-thirty in the morning. The streets were deserted. She approached the building where her husband worked. Without stopping she mounted the pavement outside the Town Hall and drove towards the plate-glass doors to the building.

Everything went into a hazy piece of slow-motion from that moment onwards. The car became a battering ram which Elaine used to rid herself of that man once and for ever.

As the plate-glass door shattered into tens of thousands of fragments, Elaine felt a hit of adrenalin that could never be matched, even by the strongest of drugs. Up until that moment her head had been like a pressure cooker but now the release valve had been activated and all the steam was surging out of her.

'Once I'd done it I felt wonderful. Something climactic had had to happen,' she admitted later.

As the car screeched to a halt in a bizarre fashion, half in and half out of the entrance to the very office that had provided her husband with the opportunity to commit adultery, the misery and black despair of Elaine Friend lifted.

'It is easy for those who have never been through a broken marriage to say sanctimoniously that they would never do such a thing,' explained Elaine afterwards. 'Secretly I think many women whose husbands have left them wish they'd had the guts to do what I did. Looking back, I have no regrets at all.'

After smashing the once-immaculate Mercedes through the glass doors, Elaine reversed it carefully out of the precinct and headed towards the nearby sea wall. The adrenalin high caused by what she had just done was still pumping through her veins and she decided to push the car into the sea as a final act of revenge against her faithless husband.

Then, just as she slowed down by the water's edge, she spotted a fisherman and decided not to go ahead with the plan. Now an even better idea came to her. Beside his flashy car, Michael's other big passion was golf. She headed straight to his golf club and dumped the car on a green, all the time thinking how Michael had regaled her with swanky stories about how he regularly played golf with the Mayor.

As Elaine ran home from the golf club in the early hours she kept thinking about Michael's face when he got to the Town Hall and saw it smashed up and she laughed out loud to herself. She was free of him.

Next day, Elaine went to the police and gave herself up. They treated her with the utmost sympathy and later, when she appeared in front of magistrates at Gosport, Hampshire, Elaine was ordered to pay £500 compensation for the damage she had caused but she was not banned from driving because of the 'exceptional circumstances' of the case.

Elaine later explained, 'As for Michael, bless him, it's all over now, and I never had as much as one complaining phone call…'

Despite everything, Elaine and Michael Friend are now blissfully reunited, living together in the same comfortable house with another new Mercedes parked outside.

# 2

'Having talked to self-confessed
violent women prisoners and former
convicted offenders, the most
immediate impression I gained is of a
relentless, uncontrollable cycle of
alternating tension, then massive
destructive energy followed by
debilitating mental and bodily
exhaustion.'

Dr Jeremy Coid, forensic psychiatrist at
St Batholomew's Hospital, London

# THE FINAL CUT

Her hair was thick, lustrous and so dark it might have been spun on the same loom as the night. Her shoulders and back were slender. The legs were just as perfect. Jaime Macias could not take his eyes off her, even though he was sitting next to his rather plump wife Aurelia at the time.

He took another swig of his beer and wondered what she would be like in bed. Aurelia studied the expression on her husband's face and knew exactly what he was thinking. She had become well used to his wanderlust, as well as to his violent attacks on her.

Having been married to Jaime Macias for almost twenty years, Aurelia had quietly accepted the suffering because she believed in the sanctity of marriage and the importance of staying together to give the children a stable upbringing.

The couple's three children – aged six months to sixteen years – looked on Aurelia as the backbone of the family. Jaime's tendency to drink and disappear for long periods had become an accepted part of life inside the Macias household.

On that particular night – 20 September 1992 – Jaime and Aurelia were attending a christening party for one of her sister's babies in an apartment just a short distance from their home in central Los Angeles, California. Even though it was a relatively formal occasion, Jaime could not behave himself.

Earlier in the evening, he knocked back some extra-strong Mexican tequila before moving back on to beers which he was consuming at an alarming rate. Aurelia was annoyed with her husband for drinking so excessively; not only was it embarrassing in front of all her relatives, but she knew that the moment they got home she would have submit to his brutal sexual demands.

Watching Jaime lusting after the attractive brunette who was dancing with a younger man particularly enraged Aurelia. She could just about cope with her husband's demands at the best of times, but to be sitting there with him while he fantasised about another woman was, she felt, incredibly insulting.

Naturally, Jaime was completely oblivious to his wife's irritated state of mind. He never once even bothered to look in her direction to see if she had noticed his obsession with the young girl.

'I'm gonna get another beer,' muttered Jaime as he got up. There was no question of asking his thirty-three-year-old wife if she was tired and wanted to go home. He was simply stating a fact to which he did not expect any response.

As Jaime wandered off in the direction of the kitchen, the girl on the dance floor gave him a brief glance. She had felt his eyes upon her as she danced with the other man and she wanted to see what her admirer looked like. At first glance, Jaime Macias, aged thirty-six, was quite a presentable-looking Latin type. In fact, it was his swarthy good looks which had first attracted Aurelia to him almost twenty years earlier.

There was no doubting the fact that Jaime noticed the girl looking in his direction because he smiled and raised his eyebrows as he passed by her. Seconds later, she broke off with her dancing partner and slipped into the kitchen.

Throughout this exchange Aurelia was watching everything. She saw the girl glance at her husband. She watched him smile back at her. She even noticed her go into the kitchen after her husband. Unfortunately, it all reminded her of how Jaime had first met her when they were teenagers back in Mexico in the early 1970s.

Aurelia considered getting up and following her husband into the kitchen but she genuinely feared that she would be humiliated if she tried to interrupt him and his new friend. In any case, there wasn't much they could do in the kitchen.

A few minutes later, Jaime emerged with a beer in one hand and the hand of the young girl in the other and they swept past assorted relatives and friends and headed straight for the dance floor. Aurelia turned her face away in disgust.

She felt the tendons in her fingers stiffen with tension. How dare he do this in front of her? How dare he call himself her husband?

She started to ask herself why she put up with his behaviour. After all these years of physical, mental and – in her eyes – sexual abuse, he was still prepared to belittle her in front of their closest associates. Why did she put up with it?

Aurelia knew that as many people were watching her response to her husband's blatant behaviour as were looking at him smooching on the dance floor. The women were infuriated. They all shared with Aurelia that same feeling of outrage. They looked in sympathy towards Aurelia. She had tears of anger and bitterness welling up in her eyes. Not once did Jaime even look in her direction. He simply did not care. Neither, it seemed, did the other smiling macho males who kept casting admiring glances in the direction of Jaime and his dancing partner.

That night something made Aurelia even more upset than usual. She started to think that it must have been the way her husband was flouting his adulterous nature right in front of her face. Usually, when he came stumbling home in the early hours stinking of cheap perfume, she could just turn her back on him in bed and ignore the obvious implications of what he had been doing.

This time it was different. She clenched her fists in tight balls of fury and got up to talk to one of her cousins, trying desperately to ignore everything that was happening around her. However, as she talked to the other woman, it became clear that she could not concentrate on what was being said. Her mind was completely focused on just one thing – a rapidly rising hatred for her husband.

She started to wonder if he would commit the ultimate insult and take this girl off somewhere intimate even though his own wife – the mother of his children – was present. Surely he would not be so blatant? She could not be sure. She suspected he had done it in the past.

By now Jaime and his new friend were dancing virtually cheek-to-cheek on the dance floor and other couples were watching and murmuring in each other's ears. Aurelia knew full well what they would be saying.

Suddenly, something inside her snapped. She marched straight up to Jaime and dragged him off the dance floor by his wrist. The men sniggered. The women looked on admiringly.

'Home! Now!' screamed Aurelia, surprised at her courage in standing up to her husband. At first Jaime looked astounded by his wife's attitude. How dare she talk to him like that – a mere woman whose place was in the home looking after their children. She had no right to tell him to go home.

Aurelia knew what was coming next.

Jaime grabbed her by the wrist and told her in no uncertain terms that he would stay at the party as long as he liked. But Aurelia's fury was still simmering and she reckoned she had nothing to lose.

'What? So you can dance with that woman?'

It was the ultimate insult to a Latino's machismo – his own wife was giving him orders. For a second he considered beating her, but then realised that it would not look good in front of an audience. Instead, Jaime held on to his wife's wrist and marched her straight out of the apartment. No one had the courage to intervene.

As the couple made their way past the rundown apartment block and clipwood, single-storey houses en route to their own home, Jaime shouted fiercely at his wife for daring to insult and embarrass him in front of family and friends. Never once did he apologise for smooching with another woman in front of her very eyes.

'How dare you talk to your husband in such a way! I ought to teach you a lesson,' shouted Jaime.

But Aurelia – who had for so long acted as a human punchbag for her husband – was not going to give in that easily.

'Teach me a lesson? You are lucky I'm still here. You don't deserve anyone.'

Aurelia fully realised by this time that the only way to avoid the inevitable beating followed by cursory sexual intercourse with her brute of a husband was to counter him on every point. Jaime was too drunk and stupid to take stock of the situation. He failed to recognise the underlying tone of his wife's voice.

By the time they finally arrived back at their cramped apartment, Aurelia had told her husband a few home truths. Strangely, she found herself becoming more and more confident. For the first time in her married life she felt as if she was actually taking the upper hand.

As Jaime began partially to sober up he should have started to take some notice but the moment they got into the flat he poured himself a huge tequila – and that was when Aurelia realised things were about to go from bad to worse.

She knew her husband was not drunk enough simply to collapse on top of the bed as he had done frequently in the past. That tequila would simply fuel his animal instincts and that would mean the nearest thing to matrimonial rape for Aurelia.

The moment they got into the bedroom, their youngest child, Jorge, started crying. Aurelia had never been so relieved to hear a child cry in her life. She believed that it would signal the end of her husband's clumsy efforts at making love.

As was often the case with Jorge, the child needed feeding so Aurelia did the thing that comes most naturally to mothers. She exposed her bosom and lay down on the bed to try to get their youngest child to sleep. Jaime had other ideas.

Within seconds of starting to breast-feed the child, Aurelia became aware that her husband was far from asleep. He was lying watching her and then he tried to fondle her. Aurelia was appalled.

'Get your hands off me, you animal!'

Momentarily Jaime stopped trying to touch his wife's breasts. Then he started running his hand further down her body. This time the tension inside Aurelia positively exploded.

'Get away from me! Get away from me!'

Jaime could not see there was any problem.

'Just do as I want, you whore!'

'You left the whore back at that party!'

Aurelia was all set to leave the matrimonial bed but then she heard Jaime snoring loudly within seconds of his last remark. Finally, the demon drink had got the better of him.

She finished feeding little Jorge and put him back in his crib. However, Aurelia was far from ready for bed. Her husband's behaviour that night had driven her to the edge of despair. She really wondered if it was worth the misery and depravity to keep their marriage intact.

As Aurelia lay next to her smelly, snoring husband she found her mind abuzz with fear and loathing. She was feeling more incensed and angry than ever before. The attempt at sex in front of their infant son was simply the final straw. She started to think about getting revenge on him for all those years of brutality and infidelity.

Her mind kept flashing back to earlier that evening when he was dancing with the other woman. She knew then and there that he must have had dozens of women since they got married. She had ignored everything up until now but now she felt an urge to get even, to make him pay for the suffering he had caused.

Aurelia slipped quietly out of bed and moved gently across the room to the tiny kitchen off the main hallway of the apartment. Her hands were not shaking; she was not in tears: she was just coldly determined. She had made up her mind.

She slid open the drawer in the kitchen cabinet and looked down at the contents. A pair of gardening shears glistened in the light pouring in from a street lamp outside the kitchen window.

Aurelia grasped the handles of the shears, lifted them out silently and walked back to the bedroom.

On the bed lay the ever-snoring heap of a human being who was her husband, her brutal, adulterous, wife-beating husband. She kept seeing rapid images of all the things he had done to her flash before her eyes.

It was blisteringly hot as evening temperatures in Los Angeles were hitting ninety degrees, so Jaime was wearing only his pyjama bottoms. He had a sheet partly covering his waist but little else.

Still grasping the garden shears, Aurelia looked down at him. She carefully opened the gap at the front of the pyjamas so that she could just make out the sight of his flaccid penis and hairy scrotum. She knelt gently and quietly on the bed next to her husband and tried to place the shears around the base of his limp member. However, they would not open wide enough, even though his member was so small and shrivelled up. She realised that it would be virtually impossible to cut it clean off in one swift move-ment. She paused to reconsider her plan of attack.

Just then, Jaime moved right on to his back in his sleep. It was a considerate move on his part for it exposed his entire genital area to Aurelia. She looked down and realised that Jaime's scrotum was actually more clearly defined than his penis, which had shrunken to such a small size.

For a moment, Aurelia tried to snap herself out of her mission to destroy her husband's manhood. Then she reminded herself of all the abuse he had inflicted on her with that thing – and thought about all the other women he had serviced with it as well. This time she was going to make him pay.

.    .    .

Jaime Macias awoke at exactly 4 a.m. with an incredible pain in his groin. Still inebriated from his mammoth drinking bout earlier, he fell out of bed and struggled in the direction of the bathroom. Switching on the light he looked down to see his pyjama bottoms soaked in blood. Then he dropped them to the floor and realised that his testicles had been completely severed.

Jaime remembers nothing else after that because he collapsed with shock at that moment. His eldest son rushed into the bathroom and immediately called the police. All the time, Aurelia looked on without making any attempt to help her husband. The look of blank satisfaction said it all. She had got her revenge...

.    .    .

The Macias separated after the attack and Aurelia was charged with corporal injury to a spouse, a felony which carries a maximum four-year prison term. Further charges of mayhem were made by LA's deputy district attorney Larry Longo after he learned of the serious nature of the injuries to Jaime Macias.

In March 1994, however, Aurelia was acquitted of the main charges against her and the jury were unable to reach a verdict on a lesser charge of battery.

Jury forewoman Claudia Marshall told the judge that Aurelia Macias had been 'verbally and emotionally abused throughout the marriage' but she denied that the jury had been swayed by the fact that Jaime wanted to drop the charges against his wife.

Aurelia's defence lawyer insisted her client should never have been brought to trial and the couple are now reconciled, with Jaime promising to mend his ways.

Footnote: Only one of Jaime Macias's testicles was recovered, and not until the day after the attack, so doctors were unable to reattach it.

# 3

'It was pure heat, which began at my toes and rushed upwards, engulfing my whole body. The urge for violence was astounding. It was automatic. I never thought about it. But the damage and the question of how I did it, as a small, slightly built girl, always terrified me afterwards.'

*Josie O'Dwyer who, when in Holloway Prison, beat up Myra Hindley in a revenge attack, leaving her senseless*

# A SENSE
# OF LOVE

Stonham Parva is the sort of hamlet where you can hear the birds singing and the trees rustling in the wind. Only a handful of cars pass through each day and the biggest event of the week is during the summer months when a cricket match is played most Sundays on the village green.

Two hundred years ago Stonham Parva provided Suffolk smugglers with a perfect stopping-off point en route inland after hauling their illicit goods ashore on the East Anglian coastline but the smugglers had long gone when teacher Vic Copperman bought one of the picturesque Georgian houses that skirt the village and decided to turn it into the Four Elms Children's Home.

Copperman's plans met with the approval of everyone

concerned, from the local council to the authorities in the south east of England and London who would provide twelve troubled youngsters. None of the locals objected as the home seemed an admirable project and the vast amount of land attached to the house meant that there would be little danger of Four Elms affecting the peace and tranquillity of the village.

The children who moved into the home were in desperate need of love, care and attention. All were from broken homes where they had either suffered at the hands of abusive parents or simply been rejected.

By the time thirteen-year-old Joanne was enrolled in the school in the early 1980s, owner Vic Copperman seemed to be running an excellent establishment. As headmistress, he had drafted in a rather over-made-up blonde called Thea Trevelyan but the authorities who used the home as a filter for their most troubled youngsters were impressed with the place.

Joanne's background was particularly tragic. As a little girl of seven she had been removed from the family home after her mother, Dee Washington, had a nervous breakdown following the break-up of her second marriage and because she simply could not cope.

Dee was riddled with guilt for failing to support her daughter but she was advised to start a new life and let Joanne settle into a home because there was a definite feeling that Dee might have further mental problems.

Dee then started to rebuild her own life. She developed an interest in shooting and became a top markswoman, even qualifying as an international referee for clay pigeon events.

However, she never forgot Joanne. She kept wondering how her daughter was surviving; what her life was like without a proper mother. Dee even went to her local authorities and asked them if she could visit her daughter with a view to maybe taking care of her again. The authorities contacted Vic Copperman at Four Elms to ask him his expert opinion as he was the only parental figure in Joanne's life at that point.

Copperman responded in an extremely sensitive way. He calmly and sensibly explained that he felt it would be ill-advised for Joanne to see her mother. Copperman told the authorities that Joanne was more settled than she had ever been before in her short and troubled life and that to reintroduce her mother for a few hours might set her development back years.

Dee was disappointed but understood the sentiments being expressed as she had suffered an unhappy, abusive childhood herself and the last thing she wanted was to add to her daughter's suffering.

Dee eventually grew to accept that it was probably best if she did not see her daughter again until she reached adulthood. It was a heart-wrenching decision but under the circumstances it seemed the only answer.

By October 1987, Joanne had grown into an attractive blonde teenager of nineteen, still in the care of Copperman and his headmistress Thea Trevelyan at Four Elms. She began to express a wish to meet her family. She was naturally curious about her background but it was decided that perhaps the best person for her to meet first would be her grandmother in Devon. A few weeks later, Joanne headed off to the West Country for a short stay.

Within days of arriving in Devon, Joanne started to drop hints about certain 'things' that had been happening at Four Elms. Her grandmother was puzzled about exactly what she meant until she laid it on the line: Joanne had been sexually abused virtually since the first day she had arrived at the children's home as a thirteen-year-old virgin.

Joanne poured her heart out to her granny and made detailed allegations about how Vic Copperman and Thea Trevelyan had involved her and other youngsters in sordid sex parties and forced her to take part in pornographic movies.

Joanne's grandmother was appalled. Not only was she shocked and horrified by what had been happening at a supposedly responsible children's home, she was angry at her daughter for allowing Joanne to be taken away from her in the first place.

The first inkling Dee Washington had of her daughter's suffering came when a stream of letters from her family arrived at her Essex home, condemning her for neglecting her daughter and revealing that poor Joanne had even attempted suicide in Devon because she could not stand the thought of returning to Four Elms.

'I just cannot believe you just stay up there doing nothing. I really am quite ashamed,' wrote Dee's sister Joan from her home in Devon.

Another letter from Dee's niece, a hospital sister who was on duty when Joanne was admitted after trying to kill herself, pleaded with Dee to come to her daughter's aid. 'Do you really not care for poor Joanne's welfare?' she asked. 'Do you not think it is time you made up for the years you neglected your motherly role?'

Not surprisingly, Joanne's grandmother and other relatives called in the police to report the teenager's allegations. Detectives reacted swiftly and positively and arrested Vic Copperman and Thea Trevelyan. They were bailed while inquiries went ahead.

It was even disclosed that, earlier, the home had come under suspicion because Trevelyan had been admitted to a psychiatric hospital suffering from severe alcohol problems. Investigations had later led to the decision, in January 1987, to withdraw children from the home – but Joanne had decided to stay on. No one knows why…

For Dee Washington, however, the die was cast. With the stinging rebukes of her family still fresh in her mind, the forty-one-year-old divorcee decided to take revenge.

Dee knew that if she was to pay back those two sick and perverted people she needed to psych herself up into a state of complete and utter contempt. She hired a video of the notorious Charles Bronson film *Death Wish*, about an ordinary man taking revenge on the men who attacked his daughter.

She sat in her house one afternoon and watched it over and over again. Each time she saw Bronson's character blast his daughter's slayers, it reaffirmed her conviction that there was only one way to avenge the abuse Joanne had suffered.

Dee carefully packed her favourite shotgun into the boot of her car and set off on the journey to Four Elms. She felt strangely calm. Her mind was made up. There was absolutely no question of turning back. Her family's criticisms were burning a hole in her heart. She bitterly regretted not taking Joanne back years earlier. She had always loved Joanne. Maybe this response would convince the rest of her family that she really did care.

Dee kept thinking back to the methods used by Charles Bronson. He never faltered. He never lost his nerve. She admired that and she was about to emulate it in every sense of the word.

On 26 November 1987, Dee arrived at Four Elms to collect her daughter's belongings. The place was deserted so she drove to a nearby town and had a coffee. The delay did nothing to lessen her determination to get revenge. When she drove back up the drive to Four Elms an hour later, Copperman and Trevelyan were standing outside.

They were a little taken aback to see Dee but soon relaxed when Dee smiled at them. Upstairs, she was shown Joanne's room which was filled to the brim with the bribes they had 'paid' Joanne in exchange for her co-operation in their sick sexual games.

They had bought her a BMX bike, a record player and records, a pedal car, dolls, stuffed toys and lots of clothes. Dee felt dreadful as she stood in that room because she knew exactly what each present must have represented.

On the surface Dee seemed calm about everything, so Trevelyan and Copperman relaxed and offered her coffee, even joking about their own predicament at the hands of the police. Copperman mentioned how much they both missed Joanne. That made Dee even angrier because she knew exactly why they missed her daughter so much.

How could these two monsters sit there and look her in the eye and even joke about their activities? It just reaffirmed her mission. Dee felt an overwhelming need to get away from them. She could not stand to listen to them a moment longer. She got up and announced that she had left something in the car outside. Copperman and Trevelyan looked relieved as she walked out. Considering they were on bail accused of sexually abusing her daughter, they were astonished at how well Dee was taking the entire situation.

Just two minutes later Dee – the one-time leading markswoman – walked back in and aimed her favourite twelve-bore double-barrelled shotgun directly at Copperman. Without uttering a word she lowered the barrel so that it was directly in line with his groin and fired twice.

Copperman crumpled to the floor in excruciating agony. Dee's intention was to make sure he never abused another child again. Those two blasts had guaranteed that.

Then Copperman started to try to crawl away.

Dee reloaded her shotgun with the ease of a crackshot, aimed the barrel at Copperman's head and fired. He could crawl no further but he was still alive. It made Dee feel better to know he was suffering. She did not want him to die too quickly.

Trevelyan – caked in make-up as usual – sat frozen to her seat throughout. She was too terrified to leave in case Dee decided to take aim at her, but it was to be her turn next.

Dee turned and pointed the gun at Trevelyan's chest. She knew that, with absolute precision, she could extinguish the life of this blonde in a split second. She squeezed the trigger and Trevelyan was no more.

. . . .

MANSION HUNT FOR GUN KILLER screamed the

headline in *The Sun* the day after Copperman and Trevelyan were shot.

> A woman was shot dead and a man seriously wounded by a crazed killer last night.
>
> Armed police cordoned off roads around a rambling mansion where the pair were found and officers started a cross-country search.
>
> Neighbours in the sleepy village of Stonham Parva, near Ipswich, Suffolk, were warned to lock doors and windows...

However, Dee Washington had completed the only killings she ever intended to commit. She was no danger to the public, only to herself.

A few hours after the killings, she nearly turned the shotgun on herself.

'I remember thinking: "To hell with it." Then a picture of my boyfriend Simon and our home flashed in front of my eyes and I did not do it.'

At the murder scene, police found Copperman near the drive of the house. He had somehow managed to crawl there after Dee's departure. As Copperman lay dying in hospital, detectives managed to extract enough information from him to establish that Dee Washington had shot both him and Trevelyan.

At twelve-thirty that night, a team of officers surrounded the house in St Osyth, near Clacton-on-Sea in Essex, which Dee shared with her boyfriend Simon Harding, aged thirty-eight. They needn't have bothered with the armed team. Dee Washington had no intention of putting up a fight. She had achieved what she set out to do and did not object when she was led out to a waiting police car in handcuffs.

The only disappointment felt by Dee was when officers told her that Copperman was still alive. 'I hope he dies because I have no feelings for him. I am not sorry I did it because of what they did to Joanne.'

Three weeks later, Dee's wish came true when Copperman died.

Dee also told the investigators, 'It was all like a dream. It wasn't real really. I didn't feel anything. I just felt disgusted at what they had done and wanted to hurt them as much as I could.'

At Norwich Crown Court, in July 1988, Dee denied murder but admitted manslaughter because of diminished responsibility. She was ordered to be detained indefinitely in a medium-security hospital after the court heard she was suffering from depressive illness.

The court was told that Copperman and Trevelyan were alleged to have lured children into wild sex-and-drink parties and there was talk of a young boy's pet rabbit being shot in front of him because he kept wetting the bed.

Former workers at the school told of often finding the drunken pair still asleep surrounded by dozens of empty spirit bottles. Bleary-eyed children would also still be in bed, recovering from wild goings-on the previous night.

Copperman was said to have groped and kissed Trevelyan during orgies in front of the youngsters. The children also spoke of weird 'war games' with loaded pistols.

A handyman once walked into a bathroom and found five youngsters watching drunken Trevelyan naked, writhing and playing with a vibrator.

Copperman's wife Pam, who ran another home called The Rookery at Stowmarket in Suffolk, later claimed, 'I have heard gossip about what went on at Four Elms but I don't believe a word of it. I knew Vic for twenty-nine years. We were childhood sweethearts. He couldn't have done anything to the children.'

Edmund Lawson QC, defending, said there was 'ample corroboration' for Joanne's allegations of sexual abuse at Four Elms. He revealed that Dee Washington had been in touch with Joanne. She also had the 'entire sympathy' of her local community in St Osyth.

The enormity of Dee's crimes could not be overlooked. 'But she did it out of a sense of love, guilt and anger.'

.    .    .

Six months after her conviction, Dee Washington was released from hospital.

Sadly, she never actually met up with Joanne, although she says, 'We are in close touch now. I speak to her on the phone every week and we write. The letter that moved me most was the one where she said she understood why I had killed Vic and Thea, and she knew it was because I loved her.'

# 4

'Women can't go into battle. I think the
very nature of women disqualifies
them from doing it. Women give life.
Sustain life. Nurture life.
They don't take it.'

*General Robert Barrow,*
*former commandant of the US Marine Corps*

# THE SEX TRAP

She was tall, blonde and very shapely. Her hair hung straight in a pleasant bob-cut. The locks seemed to bounce as she walked upright and confidently. Her eyes were wide, saucer-like seas of brilliant blue, although they sometimes seemed glazed and distant. Her hips were generous but well in proportion with the rest of her body. They gave the distinct impression that she was strong in every sense of the word; capable of taking on whatever any man had to offer, but then twenty-eight-year-old Tracey Gaywood was a very intimidating woman. She threw herself into her work as a well-paid market researcher with great enthusiasm but she always seemed to be on the edge of sadness, never quite able to sustain her success. She had similar problems in her social life. So, when she met Jeremy Parkins in 1990, she truly believed that she might have found a perfect partner. He was generous, gentle and loving, and she felt he wanted to learn as much from her as she did from him.

For five months Tracey and Jeremy enjoyed such a sexually active relationship that Tracey became convinced it was leading to even greater things, like love and marriage. Tracey really enjoyed using her body to please Jeremy. It wasn't a dirty, salacious thing to do. She saw it as deeply romantic and she liked to ensure he wanted her every night. She also knew full well that regular love making was a sure way to hold on to your man.

Jeremy – a softly-spoken twenty-nine-year-old – was completely swept off his feet at first. Tracey was the first woman he had ever met who actually enjoyed sex and was genuinely passionate. She taught him many things about the art of love and their relationship appeared to their families and friends to be safe and secure.

However, after those first months of passion began to fade, conversation between the two became a little more awkward. As the love making subsided, so did their ability to connect. Then Tracey revealed to Jeremy that she had suffered from a weight problem in the past and she also disclosed to him that she had become dangerously addicted to slimming pills when she was a little younger.

Jeremy did not take much notice until his lover started to 'act weirdly' whenever they went out together. She would twitch uncontrollably and then burst into tears. It got progressively more serious. She began talking openly of a 'demon' that haunted her. Jeremy was bemused by her claims but they definitely left him feeling a little uneasy about their relationship. Perhaps if he had been a more demonstrative fellow he might have got her to see someone to discuss her 'problem'.

In fact, Jeremy actually thought Tracey's problems were caused solely by those slimming pills. However, as the weeks turned into months it became clear that Tracey had much more serious anxieties.

One day an envelope from Tracey arrived at Jeremy's home. He recognised the writing and opened it to find a series of poems written in scraggy, erratic hand writing. The wording of the poems was disturbing, to say the least. Tracey referred to the sort of sexual acts she wanted Jeremy to perform. She seemed to be interpreting their relationship in a completely different way from Jeremy. If Tracey's intention was to improve the sexual side of their romance, then she had picked the wrong man in Jeremy. Her demands made his hair stand on end. He was starting to wonder how he had got himself involved with such a strange woman.

Soon alarm bells were ringing loud and clear in Jeremy's head. He read the poems a second time and concluded that they had to come from a very sick mind. It was time to end the relationship before it got any more serious.

It also has to be pointed out that Jeremy's departure was partly influenced by his meeting Linda Willis, a straight-talking, sane twenty-seven-year-old brunette who seemed like a breath of fresh air compared with Tracey. Linda was as sensible as Tracey was bizarre. She instantly provided Jeremy with a more secure basis upon which to have a relationship.

Jeremy – ever considerate – decided to remove Tracey from his life slowly and tactfully. He sensed that she might go completely mad if he just dropped her like a stone, so he set about gently extracting himself from her life. The warning signs of 'fatal attraction' problems kept on appearing. He needed to tread carefully, warned some of his friends.

Eventually, Tracey seemed to accept that she could not have Jeremy to herself. He had very tactfully eased himself away from her and soon they were seeing each other only very occasionally, although Jeremy did not cut the tie completely, just in case she cracked up.

What Jeremy did not realise was that Tracey was seething with anger about being dropped by him. She was thankful for seeing him every now and again but she still wanted him all to herself and she was determined not to let him off the hook that easily.

Besides becoming increasingly obsessed with Jeremy, Tracey was also in desperate need of a regular bed partner and the occasional meeting with Jeremy was not enough to satisfy her sexual demands, especially since that side of their relationship had all but disappeared. As the split between them grew more apparent, so did Tracey's determination to have Jeremy entirely to herself.

Tracey would become particularly angry on the evenings when she found herself alone in her small flat, knowing that Jeremy was probably out with *her*. She could not help thinking about what she was missing and it fuelled her burning desire to get him back.

It was during those lonely evenings in front of the

television that she started writing the most vicious, perverted poison-pen letters to Jeremy. In her mind she felt she had been betrayed by him for another woman and she wanted him back. Somehow, she convinced herself that if she promised to perform those shocking acts then he might feel he could not resist her.

When Jeremy received the letters he was even more shocked than when he got the poems a few months earlier. It wasn't just the sexual activity described that stunned Jeremy. In one letter Tracey talked about killing Linda in order to win Jeremy back. It sent a shiver up his spine.

In another letter she wrote explicit details of the sexual acts she wanted to perform with Jeremy. There was mention of bondage, rubber and leather. Unfortunately, none of it appealed to Jeremy in the slightest. Tracey seemed to be living out her weird fantasies through her letter writing. She referred to other highly explicit sex acts and they continually culminated in the death of Linda.

In her increasingly deranged and jealous mind, Tracey believed that by promising Jeremy totally uninhibited sex she could win him back. Her promise to kill Linda for him was just the icing on the cake.

Then, in January 1992, more than a year after his split with Tracey, Jeremy and Linda had a row and Linda walked out on him to stay with a friend.

For some reason, Jeremy then made a very serious error. He called Tracey up and asked if he could spend the night at her home. Whether he was lured by the promises of outrageous sex in her letters or whether he naively simply needed a place to stay, no one will ever know.

The events of that night have never been fully disclosed.

Three days later, on 2 February 1992, Tracey called her former sweetheart and suggested he call round at her flat in Barking, Essex because she had heard of a property he might want to rent nearby. Tracey was shaking with excitement when she put down the phone. In her twisted, jealous mind it seemed that Jeremy was heading right back into her arms. She decided to prepare herself for his visit in the only way she knew possible ...

Knowing she had plenty of time before Jeremy would arrive, Tracey enjoyed a long, soothing bath and thought about what would happen when he turned up. She was determined to lure him with the offer of any kind of sex he wanted. Having had a lustful relationship with him for five months, she believed she knew exactly how to turn him on and there were also a few new tricks she wanted to try out on him.

After her bath, she sprayed herself with her favourite perfume and looked through her wardrobe for her most seductive clothes. She found a tight-fitting black dress that she knew Jeremy liked and then looked through her chest of drawers for a brand-new pair of sheer black nylon panty-hose. Her attention was then caught by the thigh-high black leather boots that she knew were an instant turn-on for most men. The outfit was rounded off by a black suede jacket.

As she rolled on the tights, Tracey could hardly contain her excitement. This was the opportunity she had been waiting for. She was going to exhaust Jeremy with so much sex he would know that she was the woman for him.

Squeezing into the virtually skin-tight leather boots, she

smoothed the folds of leather over her knees just as the door bell rang. The sensuous feeling tingling through her body was almost insatiable.

The moment the door opened and Jeremy saw Tracey he knew that he was walking into a sex trap. Despite her excitable state, Tracey realised when she saw the expression on Jeremy's face that seduction would not be an instant event. However, she also had another back-up plan just in case he rejected her. For the first time she was feeling a little nervous and wasn't entirely sure what to do. Then she thought of him with that other woman. That was enough to convince her ...

She suddenly whipped out a large kitchen carving knife. Jeremy was terrified but Tracey was only just beginning. Her voice quivering with jealousy and rage at his immediate rejection, she started to talk about her rival, Linda.

'I went out last night looking for her. I would have used this on her if I'd found her,' she told the shaking Jeremy, who feared that he was about to be killed. He had to think quickly and tried calming her down. He pleaded with Tracey to leave him and Linda alone. He spoke in sensitive detail about their relationship. The glazed mask of determination and hatred on Tracey's face seemed to disappear. She looked in wonderment at her former lover and felt a twinge of sorrow for him.

When she volunteered to make them a cup of coffee, Jeremy sighed with relief. He actually seemed to have avoided a catastrophe.

Over that cup of coffee, Jeremy tried tactfully to let Tracey know that their relationship was well and truly over.

'Please stop pestering us. It's not going to make you any happier and it is not going to change things,' pleaded Jeremy.

Tracey was nodding her head in agreement as her one-time lover spoke. He believed that this might actually mean that his nightmare was over.

'OK. You're right. I will stop,' said Tracey.

Then there was a moment's hesitation in her voice. She would stop, she repeated, but only if Jeremy agreed to sleep with her and allow her to give him oral sex.

Jeremy rocked back and forth on the sofa for a few seconds and said nothing. He could not quite believe that she had just said those words. She interpreted his silence in a completely different way. A seductive smile appeared on the lips of Tracey Gaywood. She got up, walked across the room in those tight black leather boots and mini-dress and tenderly approached him, raising her arm as if to pull him towards her and kiss him. Then she looked at his unresponsive face and immediately knew. With her other hand she slipped something down the side of the sofa.

'No,' uttered Jeremy and pulled away. He felt he could not respond any other way. He did not want her.

At that moment, Jeremy felt what he thought was a punch on the left side of his neck. Then he realised that a sleek boning knife was grasped in Tracey's hand and it was covered in his blood.

Horrifically, the blade had penetrated a vital artery, causing a massive loss of blood. Bright red blood was spurting out of the side of his neck like a water fountain.

Jeremy struggled to his feet and rushed towards the

door but then he found that the door handle on the inside of the living-room door had been taken off. Tracey had deliberately removed it in order to guarantee his seduction or his death.

Scraping desperately at the spindles of the lock inside the door, he turned to see Tracey looking as she used to do after they had made love during their earlier relationship – that same expression of the cat who'd got the cream as she licked her lips with pleasure.

Still trying to poke his finger inside the spindle to release the door, he wondered if she would follow through with another knife plunge. Then he felt the blade lunging at him again and again. He tried to fend her off with one arm as he attempted to open the door with the other. Throughout all of this, blood continued to spurt uncontrollably from his neck wound.

Then, somehow, he managed to turn the lock and get the door open.

In the hallway Jeremy was greeted by a sight that summed up the sick and twisted mind of Tracey Gaywood: she had placed a chest of drawers across the front entrance.

It took all of Jeremy's rapidly diminishing strength to push that heavy piece of furniture aside and then he stumbled out into the street, screaming for help.

'Help me! Somebody help me! Please!'

Passing student Joanne Hill, aged eighteen, helped him to struggle into her home. She and her mother then staunched the flow of blood until an ambulance came to take him to hospital where doctors – who feared they were going to lose him – pulled him back from the brink of death.

As doctors battled to save Jeremy's life, detectives raided Tracey's flat but the besotted woman had vanished and was not seen for another thirteen months, when she gave herself up to an officer in London's Regent Street.

In her bedroom, police found one knife with an eight-inch blade, two with seven-inch blades, one with a four-inch blade and a claw hammer, all of which clearly indicated that there was some level of premeditation on Tracey's part.

．　．　．

At the Old Bailey in February 1994, Tracey Gaywood – a schizophrenic who once believed she was possessed by a demon – admitted wounding Jeremy Parkins with intent to cause grievous bodily harm.

The court heard that Tracey, who came from a loving family, was prescribed slimming pills at the age of fourteen after becoming obsessed about her weight. She became addicted and went on to develop severe psychotic breakdown as well as schizophrenia.

Guy Powell, defending, said, 'She is as much a victim as the man she attacked.'

Before sentencing her, Justice Brian Capstick told Tracey: 'I accept you have a loving and supportive family and that you have fallen victim of mental illness. But you deliberately used a knife intending to cause serious harm. You are fortunate the results were not more serious.'

She was ordered to be detained indefinitely in a secure psychiatric hospital until a panel of doctors is convinced she is cured.

Meanwhile Jeremy Parkins is at a secret address, still living in fear of being killed. One detective involved in the case said: 'He is terrified that if she is ever freed she will come back to get him.'

# 5

'Many women feel ripping an
expensive jacket to bits is the next
best thing to attacking the
rat himself.'

*Psychologist Tricia Kriteman*

# A STRANGE
# KIND OF LOVE

The throbbing sound of a heavy bass guitar thudded through the club and a cloud of blue smoke hung over the stage. Then she appeared, wearing a full nun's habit and balancing precariously near the edge of the raised surface, her face soft, round, yet stern, dark brown eyes staring out into the blackness in front of her. Gradually, she built up speed. Faster, faster she danced, then gave a glance across to the other corner of the dimly-lit club. She looked at her watch for a split second and then began her routine as though demons were lurking somewhere within her, her dark, swept-back hair hidden by the nun's head-dress.

Then she caught sight of him, sneering in the far corner by the bar, a beer in one hand and a cigarette in the other.

*Nun Aud Hegesanti in the habit she discarded before killing her lesbian lover's boyfriend.*

He was staring right at her and she knew precisely what was going through his mind.

As she lifted the nun's habit to reveal her long, stocking-clad legs to a murmur from the audience, she saw her best friend Bonnie sliding alongside that man by the bar. It enraged her. Sickened her. Incensed her. She ripped open the front of her outfit with fury, although to the audience of men it looked like a well-choreographed move.

Aud Hegesanti was outraged that *he* was there watching her. She was even more infuriated that Bonnie had gone up to him. It made her sick to the stomach.

'Come on. Show us more!' shouted a voice in the crowd.

That snapped her out of her bitter and twisted mood. She unhooked her bra and peeled the stockings off her legs before running them back and forth between her teeth, much to the delight of the audience.

Aud had become something of a major attraction in Oslo, Norway, not a place normally associated with strip clubs and sleazy clip joints. The reason was that her nun routine was only one step away from the truth for the buxom brunette. Only a few months previously, the twenty-one-year-old stripper had caused a hell of a stir by joining the club after fleeing from her life as a real nun in Rome.

Her story of sexual abuse at the hands of the evil elderly sisters at the nunnery made front-page news across Norway, a conservative country where such salacious goings-on rarely occur. The media were particularly fascinated by her strip routine in which she used the same habit she had worn only a few months previously to pray in. She even claimed that the way she danced for those men was similar to the type of things those awful nuns made her do as an abused teenager in Rome. It was a strip club manager's dream come true. Some nights even perfectly ordinary and respectable members of Oslo's middle class lined up at the various clubs in the hope of seeing Aud's famous routine.

However, what the papers did not mention was that Aud's vows of celibacy were soon forgotten once she joined the strip-club circuit in Norway. It transpired that the sexual depravity she suffered at the hands of those old nuns in Rome had aroused sexual preferences the young woman did not know she possessed. She rapidly became more interested in her shapely fellow dancers than in the men who filled the clubs across Oslo to see her remove her nun's habit.

The first object of Aud's genuine affection was Bonnie – a beautiful blonde dancer whose body was the envy of virtually all the other strippers she worked alongside. At first, Bonnie had been reluctant to take up Aud's offer of friendship because she had a longtime boyfriend called Klaus. However, Aud was very persistent and charming and she seemed genuinely to care about Bonnie.

Unfortunately, Bonnie feared that Klaus – who made a habit of turning up unexpectedly at the clubs where Bonnie appeared – would get very angry and beat her if she showed an interest in any other man, let alone a shapely former nun. For months she rejected Aud's continual attempts at seduction, convinced that bisexuality just wasn't her scene. But all the time she continued to feel sorry for Aud and she also knew that certain passions were being stirred every time she talked to the ex-nun.

Then one day Klaus came into a club where Bonnie was appearing and caught Aud stroking her friend's arm as the two women sat giggling at the bar between acts. He immediately realised what was happening but, instead of getting angry, he became very intrigued.

Bonnie was embarrassed and tried to explain to Klaus that Aud had never got any further than touching her arm. Klaus was disappointed and told his lover, 'I don't mind. Why don't you bring her home tonight?'

Bonnie was appalled at her boyfriend's attitude and angrily walked away from him. Later, after they were reconciled and were on their way back to Klaus's flat, he turned on Bonnie.

'What the hell is the matter with you. If she wants to make love to you that's fine by me. Just make sure I'm included.'

'You're sick,' replied a very disillusioned Bonnie.

That night Klaus would not stop going on about his wish to see his girlfriend make love with another woman. Bonnie was getting increasingly angry.

'If you don't stop it, I am going to leave. I've had enough,' she told him.

Klaus exploded. He launched into a vicious tirade about how Bonnie wouldn't even have a roof over her head if it had not been for him. And in any case what was the harm in a little innocent fun?

Bonnie shouted back at him yet again and this time Klaus smashed her in the face very hard. She fled to the spare room and refused to come out for the rest of the evening.

Next day, Bonnie was still feeling extremely bitter about the way Klaus had treated her. She hid the bruise on her face with make-up but could not hide the hurt she felt inside. She just did not like the way he wanted her to make love to Aud while he watched. It did not seem right.

At the club that evening she met Aud and told her all about Klaus's behaviour. Aud was a sympathetic listener. She told Bonnie that she respected her opinions on her own sexuality, but what had happened with Klaus was the precise reason why she preferred the company of women to men.

After their performances on stage that night, Aud asked Bonnie if she wanted to have a nightcap at her home, an isolated farmhouse on the outskirts of Oslo. Bonnie, desperate not to go home to face another night of violence at the hands of Klaus, accepted the offer, knowing full well what might happen.

Within a few minutes of getting to Aud's house, the two women were making warm, sensuous, caring love with each other and Bonnie admitted she did not know why she had put up with those sick and twisted men in the first place.

Aud was not a pushy, brutish 'bull-dyke' type at all. She had suffered so badly at the hands of those depraved nuns in Rome that she knew full well that gentle patience was

AN EYE FOR AN EYE

probably the most important single ingredient when it came to enjoyable sex.

As the two women lay together in bed following hours of passion, Bonnie started to worry about Klaus. He was virtually her pimp and she feared that because she had not gone home that night he would beat her – or even worse. He had always threatened to get her if she did not do exactly as he told her. She knew that her actions would invite very big problems.

Aud was desperate to reassure the girl she had fallen deeply in love with and made a suggestion that stunned Bonnie for a few moments – until she began to consider its implications. For Aud had said that they should lay a trap for the perverted, brutal Klaus.

'Let's give him exactly what he wants and then get him out of our lives for ever. It would be justice well done. He deserves it,' explained Aud.

The next day, Klaus looked as pleased as punch when Bonnie explained to him where she had been the previous night.

'I told you that you'd enjoy it. Now I want to come and watch next time you go with her.'

'Let's do it tonight then,' said Bonnie.

Klaus kissed Bonnie full on the lips. Just the thought of his girlfriend making love to another woman in front of him was the source of great sexual excitement. He forced his tongue into her mouth. She swallowed and did not resist because she knew she would get her revenge that evening.

That night Aud, Bonnie and Klaus enjoyed a few drinks together and some playful flirtation in the corner of the bar at the club where they were stripping before heading off for Aud's remote farmhouse.

As they got out of the taxi and stumbled up the driveway, Aud whispered in Bonnie's ear, 'Don't forget we're in control.'

Within minutes of getting inside the house, Klaus was making it perfectly clear why he had agreed to come back with the two women. He was also being particularly pushy.

'Into the bedroom now,' he grunted at them.

The two women giggled girlishly and pranced into the main bedroom. Once inside they happily performed a very private striptease for their one 'customer'.

Soon the two women were completely wrapped up in each other and virtually ignoring the panting, naked figure lying on the bed watching them.

To start with, Klaus was perfectly content enjoying his voyeuristic feast. Soon, however, he began to want more than just his own private lesbian sex show. As the two women wrapped themselves in each other, he crept quietly behind Aud and tried to have sex with her.

She immediately stopped and turned to face him.

'Get your hands off me you woman beater.'

Klaus smiled. He did not get it. He thought she was just mocking him as part of some sick and twisted sexual game. He tried to fondle her again.

'I told you! Get away!'

With that Klaus turned to his one-time girlfriend Bonnie.

'Come on, Bonnie. I want to join in.'

Bonnie did not reply. Instead she beckoned him towards

her. Both women had a glazed, deadened look in their eyes. He presumed they were inviting him to take part in an orgy. The two women played with Klaus like two kittens with a mouse. They taunted him and teased him and let him watch them only to stop their love making just before the actual moment of climax. They would not allow him to touch them. All the time the two women encouraged him to drink as many beers as he could consume. Soon he would have been incapable of sex even if they had offered it on a plate.

Eventually, Klaus's eyelids began to be more closed than open and both women knew that the time was fast approaching. When he collapsed in a drunken heap they got to work.

Klaus never even noticed Bonnie move towards him as Aud came up behind him. Bonnie sat naked in front of him just in case he awoke while Aud grasped his neck and began to squeeze. He awoke in a state of total confusion and tried to fight back, but Bonnie punched him hard in the groin and he doubled up in agony. Then she aimed a little lower. That was the place where she really wanted to inflict pain.

'We are going to teach you a lesson you'll never forget,' said Bonnie before punching him again and again.

Aud held on tight, squeezing every ounce of life out of the crumpled naked man at her feet. It was almost as if he was grovelling for his life but both women had already decided there would be only one possible outcome.

The energy was being choked out of him. The two women were breathing fast and hard now, slightly aware that a definite sense of excitement was being caused by this merciless act of violence. Neither of them felt any guilt, just quiet satisfaction that a man who expected them to perform like sex dolls at his whim was getting his just 'reward'. Moments later they extinguished the life from Klaus and toasted their everlasting love for one another in an outrageous night of love making.

Aud and Bonnie were arrested by Oslo police in November 1994, and charged with the murder of Klaus. Their trial is expected to take place in the summer of 1995.

# 6

'All I remember is this immense,
intolerable build-up of red-hot fury
and an overwhelming desire
to hurt someone I loved.
At that moment I hated him more than
anything. Then things went blank,
and after that came the shame, seeing
his injuries, his shock.'

*Judith, aged thirty-eight, a teacher who abused her
husband in revenge for the way he ignored her*

# UNDYING
# OBSESSION

Julia Wright had been looking forward to her holiday in the snow-capped mountains of Colorado for months. Her husband Jeremy had insisted she take a breather from the daily grind of bringing up four young children to help her sister celebrate her fortieth birthday. After almost fifteen years of marriage, it seemed like the perfect way to recharge one's batteries.

Jeremy had assured Julia that he would make sure the children were properly looked after, even if it meant having to take time off from his busy job as a gynaecologist in the commuter-stockbroker belt of Woking, Surrey, twenty miles from London. When Jeremy first announced that he felt Julia should take the holiday she was a trifle bemused as this

Above: *The luxurious house in Surrey where Dr Jeremy Wright lived with his wife Julia, until she decided to kill his mistress Fiona.*

Left: *Dr Jeremy Wright.*

was not exactly a regular occurrence and she was concerned about leaving the children. However, after a series of recent 'domestic problems', it certainly seemed like a very appealing idea.

Julia flew off from Gatwick Airport on that chilly day in February 1994, not realising that her away-from-it-all trip would mark the start of a tragic set of circumstances which would end in death.

From the moment she arrived in Colorado, Julia made a point of calling home every day to see how James, aged fourteen, Julia, thirteen, Felicity, nine and Sophie, seven, were coping without their mother. She was a little surprised that Jeremy was not always in but since they had hired a home help she did not worry.

On the ski-slopes of the Rockies, Julia put the pressures of her home life behind her to enjoy some sensational downhill racing. She and her sister even managed to have actual conversations without being interrupted by the children. It was all a startling contrast with family life back in England. The holiday probably marked the first occasion in years that forty-six-year-old Julia had actually managed to relax, although she never put the children out of her mind for long. Like any caring mother away from her flock, she wondered if they were coping all right without her back at the house in Heath Road, Woking.

· · ·

The envelope tucked neatly under Julia Wright's hotel bedroom door almost went unnoticed when she awoke for another day on the ski-slopes with her sister. As she bent down to pick it up, something inside her made her shiver momentarily. She had a bad feeling and she could not work out why.

A few seconds later her instincts were proved completely correct. Inside the envelope was a fax from husband Jeremy in England, informing Julia in clinical, almost business-like terms that he had moved out of their home and was living with his receptionist and close family friend, Mrs Fiona Wood.

Julia kept reading the fax over and over again in the hope that she had made a mistake and maybe it was all a bad dream. By the time she showed it to her sister, however, she knew it was deadly serious.

How could he do it? How could he just send her a fax effectively ending fourteen years of marriage? Julia kept asking herself those questions over and over again. Celebrities like Phil Collins, Sylvester Stallone and Julia Roberts might have reportedly used faxes to end their relationships, but not respectable middle-class doctors, surely?

There was the added factor of her husband's lover, Fiona Wood. Julia felt incredibly betrayed by forty-year-old Mrs Wood, whom, until a few months earlier, she had treated virtually as a sister. Mrs Wood had held a central role in the Wright family's life since taking up her secretarial post with Jeremy in 1986. Julia Wright had always had complete and utter trust in Mrs Wood, who had controlled the Wrights' lives even to the extent of organising their holidays. She had even helped Julia to book her trip to Colorado.

Certainly, there had been strong evidence in the past of a relationship between her husband and Mrs Wood but Julia had dismissed the romance as a passing phase and had – until she received that fax – been completely confident that their marriage would survive. Even when she met Mrs Wood's husband Peter and he had told her of the affair, she had chosen to bury her head in the sand and wait patiently for it to burn itself out. Julia was determined to rescue this situation as she believed there was absolutely no need to flush fourteen years of marriage and a large happy family unit down the drain.

Jeremy had actually begun his romance with Fiona when

they both went to a medical conference in Washington DC the previous year. The affair had caused a lot of stress and strain for both families even before that fax arrived in Colorado and Julia's initial response had been to start behaving very erratically. In effect, she suffered a virtual nervous breakdown because of her husband's behaviour.

Just before Christmas 1993, Julia suddenly walked out of the family home without reason. A few hours later she rang from a phone box at Hatton Cross tube station, about fifteen miles away, offering no explanation for her strange behaviour but asking to be picked up and brought home. There had been another incident when she ran out of the house barefoot and sprinted over to a neighbour's home in tears.

Then, on New Year's Day, Julia made a bizarre plea for help by attempting suicide after downing pills and driving her car at high speed at the garage doors of their home, while clutching photos of her family. The following day she also tried to gas herself in the fume-filled garage.

In hospital the day after that incident, a doctor was called and advised psychiatric admission to a special hospital. Julia kept repeating to the doctor that her life was not worth living if she could not keep her husband. There was no hatred for Jeremy, just an obsessive insistence that the family had to stay together. It was further fuelled when one of the couple's daughters let slip that Mrs Wood had taken the children to the cinema while Julia had been in hospital. How dare *she* take over my role as mother, thought Julia.

With all this in mind, Jeremy Wright decided to remain

at the family's £500,000 detached home, which gave poor Julia the impression that he would end his relationship with Fiona Wood. Julia saw it as a victory – she had won back her husband. She never once admonished him for having the affair in the first place. She believed that his relationship with Mrs Wood was entirely the fault of that 'other woman' who had become one of her best friends and then secretly plotted to break up her family.

By the time Julia's holiday in Colorado came around, she was convinced that things at home were back on the straight and narrow or else she would never have made the trip. She actually believed that she had saved her marriage.

·   ·   ·

Within minutes of receiving that cold-hearted fax in America, all of Julia fears, anger, resentment and fury came flooding back. Throughout all of this, she remained steadfastly loyal about her husband's actions even though others in the family considered him to be an emotional coward. Meanwhile, her incredible resentment towards Mrs Wood, the 'home-wrecker', continued to grow at an alarming rate.

Within minutes of arriving back at their home after that disastrous holiday, Julia rushed into the couple's en suite bathroom, snatched her husband's bathrobe off a door hook and starting smothering it with hugs. The tears were flooding down her cheeks. She could not lose him. She would not lose him. Nobody was going to take him away from her.

The following month – March – there was little surprise among close family and friends when Julia Wright attempted suicide for the third time. However, that particular plea for help unwittingly allowed her husband to move his mistress into the family home. For while Julia was recovering after trying to take her own life, Fiona Wood was at the Wright home looking after her lover's children. It was a situation guaranteed to inflame Julia's manic determination not to lose her husband. She also became deeply paranoid that Mrs Wood wanted to take the children away from her as well.

Within days of getting back home, Julia started to make it her business to find out as much as possible about her husband's illicit affair. She wanted to know precisely when it started; how often they had been together; what Jeremy's life was like now that he had moved into a house with Mrs Wood; what sort of cottage the illicit lovers had rented in nearby Cobham. She investigated the subject in much the same way as an author researches a book.

Julia even discovered a series of endearing messages left on her husband's bleeper by Mrs Wood. They were overtly romantic and reminded her of the courtship she had enjoyed with Jeremy all those years earlier, before she had given up her job as an anaesthetist to bring up their family.

Julia also started turning up at odd hours in Jeremy's surgery – the North Surrey Laser Centre – on an industrial estate near their home. On one occasion she discovered a letter he had written to Mrs Wood, saying that he loved her more passionately than anyone else. That letter shattered all Julia's illusions. The loving sentiments expressed in the note finally convinced her that her marriage was in dire trouble. Julia had literally made herself mentally ill through the stress and anger caused by her marriage break-up. Now she had to face reality.

She had given up her career to devote herself entirely to her family. Nothing else had mattered in her life. She loved her husband beyond measure and, as she saw it, he had been taken away from her and her children by another female – a woman once known to the family as 'the lovely Fiona'.

Julia's inner turmoil was twisting her mind into a contortion of hatred. One night she paged her husband at his love nest to ask him out for dinner. When he did not even bother to reply she interpreted his lack of response as having been caused by her rival for his love. She still believed that her husband was totally faultless and told friends that she would take him back at the drop of a hat. Some tried to convince Julia to get on with her life but she wouldn't hear of it. Jeremy was her life.

The following day Julia was driving her children to school through the centre of Woking when, by complete chance, she saw her husband and his lover as they passed each other in traffic. Julia was transfixed by them. She watched their every move as her husband's car drove slowly past and what she saw made her lose control of her senses. They were chatting and laughing together as if they did not have a care in the world; as if they were the happily married couple. Julia's eyes met those of her husband's lover for a split second. She never did discover if Fiona had seen her that morning.

'Fiona was sitting in the front seat and had a horrible triumphant grin on her face,' Julia later recalled. Going through Julia's mind was that *she* was muscling in on her children and she wasn't going to let her take her children as well. The two pillars that supported Julia Wright's life were the love of her husband, whom she believed could do no wrong, and the love of her four children.

As Julia continued to watch her husband and his lover in the traffic that morning, she felt a surge of anger and crunched her hands tightly round the steering wheel. She convinced herself that Mrs Wood was about to take over her family as well as her husband.

A few minutes later, Julia arrived at her children's school in tears and grabbed hold of a friend's arm. She told her: 'I have just seen them together... I cannot cope.'

After dropping the children off, Julia drove home immediately. This time she was going to do something about it. She could not sit back and watch that woman take her family away from her.

She walked straight into the kitchen, ripped open a drawer and took out a five-inch Kitchen Devil knife which she had bought just a few weeks earlier. She turned around, marched straight back out to the car and drove directly to Jeremy's private surgery in Westminster Court, Old Woking, where she knew Mrs Wood would be working.

Julia stormed in and yelled at her husband's mistress, 'You ruined our lives!'

Fiona Wood stood by with a bemused smile on her face.

'Do you realise how many people you have hurt?' ranted Julia.

Mrs Wood just laughed and muttered, 'It's mutual.'

The last thing Fiona Wood wanted was a confrontation

with her lover's wife, especially as she was well aware that Julia had been becoming increasingly deranged over the previous few months.

Now Julia was being taken to the edge once again. It did not need much to push her over. She kept thinking of the children being looked after by *that woman*. It was enough of an incentive.

Suddenly Julia lashed out at Mrs Wood with her fists, punching her in the face several times. Then she produced the knife. 'You will not get my children. You will not get my children.'

She uttered the words over and over again.

Suddenly Julia lunged at the face of the woman who had lusted after her husband and entrapped him. She slashed at Mrs Wood's eyes and mouth eighteen times. There was blood everywhere. As her body crumpled to the floor, Julia stabbed the life out of Mrs Wood with another seventeen wounds.

'This is what happens to trusted friends who seduce husbands and wreck marriages and families,' Julia thought to herself. This was what happened to scarlet women who attend the same country church and teach at the same Sunday School while all the time scheming to have an affair with her husband.

By the time all those thoughts had passed through her mind, there was nothing left of Fiona Wood. She was a twisted, bloodied heap on the floor of the surgery where she and her doctor lover had initiated their romance.

Mrs Wood's body was so badly mutilated that she could only be identified later through dental records.

Julia felt elated by her achievement. Now she could repair the marriage and start again. She walked out of that office with her head held high.

The only other people in the building that morning heard several short screams and then silence, with one exception.

Julia – covered in the blood of her victim – ran up the hall to her husband's consulting room. She threw open the door and rushed into Jeremy Wright's arms.

'Everything is all right now. You can come home. I have killed her. She is a wicked woman who has taken you away from your family.'

.    .    .

Julia Wright admitted the manslaughter of her husband's secretary and mistress, Fiona Wood, on the grounds of diminished responsibility when she appeared at the Old Bailey in December 1994. She had denied murder.

Mr Julian Bevan, defending, told the court: 'She attached no blame to her husband. She saw him as a victim. Others might not be so generous.'

Since her arrest, he added, she had recognised 'that her life with Jeremy is over. She did not recognise that at the time.'

Mr Bevan said he would be misleading the court if he said she expressed any remorse for Mrs Wood but she was remorseful about the consequences for her victim's family.

The judge, Mr Justice Blofeld, said he sentenced her on the basis that medical reports concluded that she was not a danger to Mr Wright or anyone else with whom he was associated.

He said she bore a 'substantial residual responsibility' and had 'no sensible reason' to act in the way she did. Julia admitted manslaughter on the grounds that depressive illness had impaired her sense of responsibility. She was jailed for four years.

Three of Julia's children were in the court to see their mother sentenced. They looked down from the public gallery as the white-faced woman, wearing a navy twin-set, was led from the dock to start her sentence in Holloway Prison. The oldest, James, waved and smiled and mouthed 'goodbye'.

The Rev. James Song, former vicar of the church in Woking which the Wrights and the Woods had attended, and who conducted Mrs Wood's funeral, said after the case:

I had known Fiona Wood for about ten years and although she was a very popular person and a regular worshipper, she gave up her Sunday School teaching and her attendance at church tailed off about eighteen months before the attack. I think this was the time the affair started and she found it difficult to reconcile the two.

Fiona Wood was a hard-working, very attractive woman who lived on an estate and rose to the level of working for an eminent man – setting out his diary, running his life and organising parties and gatherings at Glyndebourne. She was given access to an affluent lifestyle.

Mr Wright had felt his marriage to have been dead for a while. She lent him a supportive ear – they talked together, then started going out for meals and from there the affair started.

She knew what she was doing. We live in the 1990s and we accept that people fall in love all the time. It is the easiest thing in the world to happen.

It [the funeral] was one of the saddest things I have ever had to do. Peter Wood was there, of course, and behind him sat Mr Wright, who had also lost someone. One of Mr Wright's children was there because they had known Fiona well.

At the end of the ceremony I was with Peter as he said goodbye to those who had attended and he shook Jeremy Wright's hand and spoke to him.

Peter behaved like the perfect gentleman. Even though their marriage had ended, the funeral fell on his shoulders. Both Peter Wood and Jeremy Wright started going to the church after the funeral. In the end the people who knew and loved Fiona were faced with the same feeling of loss.

After the case, Fiona Wood's husband Peter, a forty-four-year-old marketing executive, talked about his twenty years of married life with her and about their two teenage children. 'This case has brought into focus the loss that I and my family have suffered.'

He said that although he and his wife were separated at the time she was killed, they had remained on friendly terms.

He added: 'She was a lovely lady and a good friend. She was very popular.'

Jeremy Wright's mother said after the trial, 'You have to feel sympathy for someone, however deranged, who felt the need to do something so dreadful. It didn't solve any problems. The ripples it has caused are endless. No one knows where it is going to end.'

.    .    .

Jeremy Wright started a new relationship with another woman just six weeks after his wife killed his mistress. He has not spoken to Julia Wright since the attack.

His solicitor, defending his client's decision to start another affair so soon after the tragedy, said: 'I understand there has been criticism of him but he does not wish to answer that. He is simply interested in getting on with his life. What people think is not important.'

# 7

*'May you not hurt your enemy when
he struck first?'*

**Aeschylus, The Libation Bearers *(458 BC)***

# FATAL
# ATTRACTION

Driving instructor Ancell Marshall was renowned as a very calm character who took everything in his stride. He had a friendly demeanour but he never wavered from the job at hand. He firmly believed in gently coaxing his pupils so that they gained confidence, and then driving skills would naturally follow.

Ancell even prided himself on never having raised his voice to a pupil. Certainly there had been moments when his life seemed in peril but Ancell had always calmly taken over the controls and avoided disaster. In the words of one of his fellow teachers, he was 'a complete professional'.

So when attractive brunette Rene Sampat enrolled for a series of lessons, Ancell understandably presumed that he

*Rene Sampat, who killed the wife of the man she became obsessed with.*

was about to embark on another successful mission to teach someone how to drive. When Rene got in the driver's seat to begin her first lesson, Ancell gave no thought to the friendly smile on her face or the momentary flash of thigh that she provided while adjusting her position.

Ancell made it a strict rule not to talk too much to pupils, fearing it might distract them from their concentration on driving. That day, however, Rene kept asking him questions and she had the unfortunate habit of turning to talk to him rather than looking ahead at the road.

'Please keep your eyes on the road,' was about the strongest remark mild-mannered Ancell ever made. Other instructors might have been a little more blunt but Ancell believed he had a duty not to be in any way offensive to his pupils.

Rene completely ignored Ancell's request and just kept on talking, but then that was typical of Rene Sampat. Every time they stopped at a junction or traffic lights, she would turn and smile in his direction. Ancell began to notice all this but did not want to acknowledge her actions because he felt it might seem rude of him.

As Rene pulled up at the end of the lesson, Ancell felt a rather strange atmosphere. He couldn't quite put his finger on it but as a man of the world he had a horrible inkling of what was about to occur.

As he turned to get out of the car, Rene engaged Ancell in yet another banal conversation. The next thing he knew her hand was on his. He couldn't quite work out if she was making a pass at him or just being over-grateful for her lesson. He pulled his hand away and ignored the entire incident.

Ancell watched Rene walk off down the street after that lesson and decided that perhaps she did seem rather forward. On the other hand, he was probably imagining it. As a lay preacher at the Seventh Day Baptist Church in Victoria Road, Tottenham, north London, he preferred to think the best of people and tucked all other thoughts away into another part of his mind. He was actually rather annoyed with himself for even suspecting Rene's motives that day.

The following week Rene turned up for another lesson and this time she looked as if she was dressed up for a evening out at a casino. Jewellery was glittering from every finger and she had such a vast pair of earrings that Ancell wondered if they would interfere with her driving capabilities.

Just as on the previous lesson, Rene made all the conversation, despite Ancell's occasional – and highly apologetic – requests for her to keep her eyes on the road. That smile seemed to be permanently painted on Rene's face whenever she looked in Ancell's direction. It was finally dawning on him that perhaps Rene did have other things on her mind besides driving.

A few minutes before the end of that lesson, Rene Sampat tried to fondle Ancell, lost control of the car momentarily and almost crashed. To this day, Ancell has been too embarrassed to say precisely what happened but he immediately told Rene that it would be better if she was taught by another instructor.

Ancell Marshall presumed that would be the end of his association with Rene. In fact, it was only just the beginning.

.　　.　　.

Ancell got quite a surprise when he was showing congregational members to their seats one Sunday and divorcee Rene – the driving-school pupil from hell – turned up, accompanied by three of her younger children.

He gulped but acted calmly and courteously. He did not know that thirty-three-year-old Rene – a mother of five – had joined the Seventh Day Baptist Church despite being a committed Muslim. Just a few months later, he began to discover why.

'You'll have to go and see her. She's asked for you by name, Ancell,' one of Ancell's fellow lay preachers at the church told him by phone one evening.

It transpired that Rene Sampat had contacted the church asking that lay preacher Ancell should visit her home to counsel her following an incident that had occurred. Ancell's colleague said it sounded pretty serious and he had a duty to investigate.

When Ancell knocked on the front door of Rene's home in Seaford Road, he was feeling very apprehensive but the trusting side of his nature told him not to make any prejudgements. This lady had said she had been attacked and she needed gentle patience, not a suspicious response from a man who feared that her intentions might not be entirely honourable.

He sat and listened to her story of having been raped by a stranger and recommended that she call in the police, but she refused. Ancell left her home that evening rather bemused by the whole story. Nothing was ever mentioned about it again.

Then, a few months later, Rene phoned Ancell at midnight when he was in bed with his wife Jannette, just about to go to sleep. This time Rene was in tears. She told him she had been raped again and gagged and tied up and could he come round and untie her.

Ancell took a deep breath and advised her to call the police, but she refused. Again, the incident was never mentioned again, although Ancell did feel a little worried about Rene's motives in calling him in the first place.

When Ancell was told by his colleagues at the church to go round to Rene's house following a third rape allegation he became extremely apprehensive about whether he should even be going there.

Within minutes of arriving at the house, Rene burst into tears and then tried to kiss Ancell. All Ancell's worst nightmares were coming to fruition. He immediately pulled back from Rene, but she then collapsed at his feet and pleaded with him to go to bed with her there and then.

Ancell was totally confused. He could not understand how a woman would make very serious claims of rape in one breath and then ask for sex with a happily married man the next moment. He kept reminding her of his married status and the position he held in the church but Rene's obsession was not that easily extinguished.

Ancell once again advised Rene to go to the police

about her rape allegations. She ignored him and insisted on talking about what they could do in bed together.

Soon afterwards, Ancell left the house in a very confused state. He knew that any involvement with Rene would be certain to lead to even greater problems but as a lay preacher he genuinely believed that he had a duty to help her. It was hardly as if he could go to the police about her. They had more important things to deal with than a lay preacher claiming that a woman was trying to seduce him!

Rightly or wrongly, Ancell decided to let sleeping dogs lie. His only concern was to get on with his life as a driving instructor, responsible husband to a quietly-spoken wife, and father to their three children.

However, Rene was still desperate to lure Ancell into her web of seduction so she took Ancell's advice and called the police to her home in nearby Stoke Newington after another alleged 'attack'. She hoped that their involvement might actually convince Ancell that she needed sympathy and understanding.

Officers who arrived at the house were bemused to find Rene still naked and tied up. She told them a man had climbed in her window and asked her 'to do all sorts of things to him' at knifepoint.

Then, after the officers had untied her, Rene ran into the kitchen of the flat and tried to stab herself after one of the detectives suggested she might be lying. Rene only calmed down after a policeman said he had powers to take away her children if she continued acting in such an erratic manner.

Some months later, Ancell got a call from his father

who also attended the same church in Tottenham. He had some disturbing news: Rene Sampat had been to visit him and had pleaded with him to convince Ancell to have an affair with her.

Ancell was shocked. His father went on to explain that Rene kept going on and on about it to him. She even said she did not want to marry his son, just to 'have a relationship with him'.

Ancell was completely astounded. How could a grown woman – and mother of five children – go and see his father and talk in such an obscene manner? It all seemed unreal and for that reason Ancell decided to do nothing about it. He did not confront Rene. He did not even act any differently when he saw her in church each Sunday. He had decided that, as the Lord's servant, he had to show compassion and forgiveness towards her. That meant making an extra-special effort to be kind to Rene just to make sure she did not feel hurt. In retrospect, Ancell Marshall should have nipped the entire situation in the bud, but he did not.

By 1987, Rene had become remarkably generous towards not only Ancell, but his entire family. Ancell was convinced that all that 'confusion' earlier had been forgotten, and if anything, Rene was trying to show that she wanted to be a genuine friend. She even sent Ancell a seventy-pound overcoat, as well as countless gifts for his family.

And Ancell – being a highly religious and forgiving man – tried to show how much he now trusted Rene by allowing her to look after his children whenever Jannette was out working. He had no idea that she was only prepared to look after the youngsters because it gave her an opportunity to ingratiate herself with the man of her dreams.

When Jannette Marshall celebrated her birthday that year, Rene even persuaded a friend of the family to lend her the key to their flat so that she could prepare a surprise meal for Jannette and decorate a room as part of the celebrations.

Ancell was delighted by this apparent about turn on the part of Rene. All the sexual innuendo and obscene suggestions from earlier days had been completely put behind them both. He even noticed that his wife was growing increasingly fond of Rene.

However, Rene's mind was still filled with wild fantasies concerning Ancell. She was perfectly happy to put on a façade in front of his wife, just so that she could be near to the man who she actually believed could give her everlasting happiness. Sometimes she found herself admiring him secretly from head to toe at church functions. She memorised every single detail of his body and stored it in her mind so that she could visualise them in bed together whenever she wanted.

Ancell occasionally caught a lingering glance from Rene but dismissed it as simple friendship, although it definitely did bother him. One time, she brushed past him in the kitchen at their home and, for a split second, he felt her quickening breath. Then the moment passed.

By the winter of 1988, Rene's sexual fantasies about Ancell were bordering on the dangerously obsessive. She decided that if she could not have Ancell as her secret lover, she would start a campaign to have him entirely to herself.

During a holiday in Tunisia, Rene confessed to a

girlfriend – who was also a close friend of the Marshalls – that she would marry Ancell if anything ever happened to his wife. The friend was shocked by Rene's open admission of lust for Ancell.

Rene knew precisely what she was doing. She wanted to make sure her thoughts were conveyed to Mrs Marshall. She then decided to stir up even more trouble by insisting to the friend she had had an affair with Ancell and become pregnant but had had an abortion.

It was all so detailed that the friend believed her. In fact, Rene had been fantasising for so long about her 'life' with Ancell that she had virtually begun to believe in her own lies, making them sound even more convincing.

Rene openly longed to have Ancell to herself. She was also desperate to have a child by him as that would seal their 'love' for one another. In her imagination she had married him already. She could visualise them making love together; bringing up children; living in a wonderful house. It would all have made a perfect Mills and Boon fantasy if it had not been so tragically misguided.

Rene's sad and twisted vision of her imaginary life with Ancell came crashing down in September 1989, when Jannette Marshall became pregnant with her fourth child. The reality of what was happening suddenly dawned on Rene and she became very angry and vindictive. How could he do such a thing to her? How could he betray her by having another child by that woman?

In Rene's mind it should have been her having that baby by Ancell. She looked on Jannette's pregnancy in much the same way a wife would look upon it if her husband's mistress was having a child. Rene believed she was the wife and Jannette was the other woman. She was starting to lose touch with reality.

A stream of nasty, vindictive, threatening, poison-pen letters began arriving at Ancell Marshall's home. He suspected they were coming from Rene but could not be sure. Jannette Marshall was naturally upset and very concerned that such a vicious person should embark on a highly personal campaign against them.

What made them doubly bizarre was that some of the letters were signed by someone calling themselves 'Erek' and they suggested that the child Jannette Marshall was carrying was a result of an affair with 'Erek'. The letter went on to insist that Jannette preferred 'Erek' to Ancell and read: 'When you touch her body she says it feels like a snake. You breath stink. You cannot kiss good.'

Another letter claimed 'Erek' had made love to Jannette in the family home and even left a condom in the toilet.

At the Seventh Day Baptist Church, Rene secretly daubed graffiti on a wall, saying that 'Erek' was the father of the couple's latest child. People were starting to talk. Was there something going on between Rene and Ancell after all? Her campaign was starting to make inroads into his otherwise happily married life.

Ancell was stunned. How could Rene Sampat go to such extremes? But then, perhaps it wasn't her after all. He was very confused by the entire situation but still Ancell refused to go to the police, preferring to hope it would all blow over.

By the time the baby was born, the Marshalls were in

an understandably distressed state as the letters continued to arrive with alarming regularity. Each time they would get more obscene.

Then one letter turned up containing the ominous threat that Jannette would die on the first birthday of the child. Ancell read it and, yet again, chose to ignore it. No one knows why Ancell never actually confronted Rene about his suspicions concerning those poison-pen letters. Instead, he allowed Rene to continue to step in and out of his life. He even hired her to cook food for a takeaway restaurant he ran as a sideline to his driving school.

In the middle of April 1991, Ancell actually visited Rene's home to collect some food she had cooked for his restaurant. For Rene, having Ancell in her home was too good an opportunity to resist. Soon, she was trying to kiss and embrace him. Ancell used the tray of food he had just picked up to push her away but Rene tried to hold him and kiss him on the mouth, pushing her tongue between his lips.

'What is the matter with you?' said Ancell and pushed her away.

Rene felt humiliated by his rejection. She had actually presumed that by coming to her house he was finally going to consummate their love for one another. She had never doubted that they would end up making love that evening. She had worked it all out in her fantasies. Instead Ancell had rejected her in a cruel and callous manner.

She decided there and then that the only way to have him for herself would involve a carefully planned scheme to get rid of her rival for his love. She began to construct a story that would guarantee her revenge on her rival.

AN EYE FOR AN EYE

At her home in Seaford Road, Tottenham, Rene broke down in tears one evening and poured out her problems to her sixteen-year-old son Roy. She insisted she had been raped by a man who was ordered to attack her by Jannette Marshall. She recalled vivid details of the 'attack' and of how jealous Jannette had sworn revenge on her because of her close relationship with Ancell Marshall.

'We have to pay her back for what she has done,' Rene told Roy.

Like any good son, Roy was appalled at what his mother was saying. He agreed that they had to do something to get back at Jannette Marshall for causing this horrific attack on Rene.

She kept repeating over and over again how terrible it had been to be raped and that no one should be allowed to get away with it. Rene was cleverly manipulating the situation by playing on her son's emotions. Soon he had worked himself up into a lather of hatred for Jannette Marshall and could not wait to go round to her home and see that 'justice' was done.

On 28 April 1991, a few days before the baby's first birthday, Rene called Ancell at his takeaway restaurant and pleaded with him to visit her. 'You must call round here before you go home.' Rene was most insistent. It bothered Ancell because, despite all of her bizarre behaviour over the previous six years, she had never before been so pushy about getting him to go round to her home. However, after what had happened on the previous occasion, Ancell refused and, instead, went home to his wife Jannette and their children.

The house was pitch-dark by the time Ancell arrived

home. An eerie silence enveloped the hallway. He walked into the sitting room and flicked on a light switch.

Lying on the floor was the lifeless body of his wife, Jannette. She had been strangled, beaten and stabbed fifteen times. The blanket covering her was caked in blood. Ancell was horrified. He rushed to gather up the couple's children, aged ten, eight, seven and eleven months, and then went outside and called the police on his mobile phone.

.    .    .

At the Old Bailey, in October 1993, Rene Sampat was jailed for life for the murder of Jannette Marshall. Her sixteen-year-old son Roy Aziz had carried out the murder after she 'manipulated and inflamed' him with false claims that the dead woman had got a man to rape her. Roy had earlier been convicted and ordered to be detained in youth custody.

Their conviction brought to an end a lengthy ordeal for Ancell Marshall, who had been arrested and had stood trial for the murder of his wife at the same court in February 1992. He was released halfway through the hearing when the judge ruled that there was no case for him to answer. Tragically, he had been refused permission to attend his wife's funeral while in custody awaiting trial.

Rene had been a prosecution witness against Ancell but a fresh police investigation uncovered the depth of her obsession, together with evidence which pointed to her hand behind the murder.

Prosecuting counsel Nigel Sweeney said at the trial: 'She was the person with the motive to set it [the murder] up. She was infatuated with him and tried in various ways over a number of years to win him over, without success. She determined that Jannette Marshall should be murdered so that Ancell could be hers.'

Ancell Marshall whispered 'amen' as the jury gave their verdict. Outside the court, however, he had to be given police protection when he was bombarded with stones by a mob supporting Rene Sampat.

He said: 'I am elated and satisfied that justice has been done. It won't bring my wife back but it was necessary that those who have committed this evil act on my wife should be brought to justice.'

Deeply religious Ancell added that he felt a 'divine intervention' had been present throughout the case. 'I feel to a certain extent it was almost necessary for me to have been treated in that manner ... almost as a scapegoat ... in order that the real person or persons responsible should be brought to justice. My prayers have been answered and I knew God would vindicate me over the horrible and nasty smear that has been said about me.'

Ancell claimed he had no idea that Rene was obsessed with him. 'She is demonic and evil. She is wicked. She has referred to an obsession but I can only sum it up as saying that she has been used by the Devil.'

Ancell and his daughters Charlene, now thirteen, Naomi, now eleven, Stacey, seven and three-year-old Rebecca are currently living with his mother in another part of Tottenham.

'I often wonder why our family had to suffer this. But we're in God's hands. He must have had a reason to allow it,' he added.

Detective Superintendent Gavin Robertson, who led the investigation, said: 'The sort of woman who can plan the death of a mother of four who had never done her any harm, and use her own sixteen-year-old son to do it, is beyond words.'

Rene Sampat's QC, Mr Graham Boal, told Mr Justice Richard Lowry: 'You may think it has been realistically described as a fatal attraction and you may think it can also be described as a fatal obsession.'

As Rene Sampat was led to the cells she shouted out: 'I am not guilty of murder. I am guilty of love.'

# 8

'In taking revenge, a man is but even
with his enemy; but in passing
it over, he is superior.'

*Francis Bacon, Essays (1625)*

# THE ONLY
# ANSWER

When eleven-year-old Karen Bigham heard her twelve-year-old brother Paul let out another cry, she trembled with fear, too scared to say anything as she lay in her bed. She hoped and prayed that the beating had finished, that their bullying stepfather had ended his violent tirade against the boy.

Karen looked across as Paul came into the room weeping and snivelling following the attack he had suffered at the hands of vicious, twisted Archie Bigham, and wondered how it had all ended so cruelly for them.

Only a few years earlier, in 1979, the brother and sister had been delighted when Archie formally adopted them after marrying their mother Terri. It meant they had a father again. By 1987, however, Archie and Terri had split up and a tragedy was about to unfold.

The first piece of bad luck occurred when there was a fire at the house Karen and Paul shared with their mother in the Essex seaside town of Southend. The property was gutted and while Terri looked for another home, the children had to move into their adopted father's house in nearby Barking.

At first things had been all right, but then Archie Bigham had started beating young Paul. That was just the beginning.

Not content with inflicting terror on Paul, Archie also turned his attentions towards little Karen. Too scared to do or say anything, she was forced to take part in sick and perverted sexual acts which effectively stole her childhood from her.

The confused schoolgirl could not understand why he was doing these dreadful things. Her confidence was gradually shattered by the relentless nature of his molestations. The man she had admired for so long was betraying her trust and hurting her both physically and mentally.

Every time Bigham entered a room in that house, Karen feared he was about to inflict more pain and suffering. The abuse went on for many months and Karen began to withdraw into herself more and more, all the time building up a reservoir of hatred and resentment for that evil man who still insisted on calling himself her father.

At one stage she began to wonder if it was all her fault. Maybe she had invited his perverted lust? Perhaps she had caused it all? All the classic feelings of guilt began to dominate her thoughts. The worst aspect of all was that the fear and shame had combined to persuade Karen not to reveal the horrific attacks to anyone. Such is the shame suffered by victims of abuse.

At night, Karen would cry herself to sleep. Sometimes she even hoped she would not wake up again the next day. When she did wake, there was an overriding feeling of disappointment that everything had not been just a dreadful nightmare. The reality became harder and harder to cope with.

Karen had few friends at school because she had become so withdrawn. Some teased her because they thought she was timid. If only they had realised what anguish she was going through.

It was not until Karen reached her teens that she even allowed herself the luxury of thinking that perhaps all those attacks had not been her fault after all. It took a tearful admission to her mother Terri to make her realise that *he* was the monster and that *he* should be punished for inflicting such harm on an innocent child.

Terri was understandably appalled when she heard from Karen what had happened. She felt a real sense of betrayal by the man who had at one time seemed like the perfect father to her children.

Within hours of hearing Karen's horrific account, Terri visited her local police station and initiated an investigation into the activities of Bigham. Afterwards, she consoled the terrified Karen by assuring her that soon that animal would be locked up where he could not cause her or any other children any harm.

Karen hoped that the cloud of fear would diminish. Maybe for the first time in years, she might feel she could enter into a friendship without worrying that it might end up as an act of betrayal like the ultimate sin that had been committed on her by Bigham.

For any sexually abused child the most difficult aspect is to try to get on with one's life. To try to start to rebuild confidence in other people after such a dreadful crime has been perpetrated. Karen believed that, finally, she might actually have a life to look forward to.

In March 1991, when Karen was fifteen, Archie Bigham finally appeared before a judge at Snaresbrook Crown Court in east London, to face charges. Looking shamefaced after hearing the sordid details of the attacks he had inflicted on his stepdaughter, he pleaded guilty to three charges of indecently assaulting Karen and asked for eleven other offences to be taken into consideration.

Karen was elated. At last she felt that justice had been done. All those years of never being able to get that monster out of her mind might now be coming to a close. The man who'd scarred her life was about to be locked away for a long time. Or so she thought.

Somehow – even though Bigham had admitted being a repeated child molester – he was sentenced to just three years' probation.

Sitting in the court waiting to see him given what he deserved, Karen was astounded. This was the man who made her do things that no child should ever have to endure. This was the man who felt absolutely no remorse for his perverted habits. This was the man who had ruined her life.

Karen put her head in her hands when it was explained to her that probation meant Bigham would not serve one day in prison. He was free to walk from that court. He was free to come back and haunt her and he was free to molest and abuse other youngsters.

The fact that the court insisted he behave himself for the next three years or face being slung into jail meant nothing to Karen. The fact of the matter was that her stepfather had been simply slapped on the wrists for being a paedophile. Where was the justice in that?

As Karen seethed over the lenient sentence, she felt almost as much hurt as she had during all those long months of sexual torture and abuse. Would the nightmare ever end? Karen promised herself she would resolve the situation some-how, even if it meant having to resort to her own brand of justice.

In July 1991, she devised a plan. She knew the precise movements of her evil stepfather and she was going to make him suffer. As he walked in the street one day, she and a friend ambushed and attacked Bigham. She could see in his eyes that he knew full well why they were after him. He put up no resistance as he was left reeling in the street after two crushing blows to the head.

Karen warned him never to do what he did to her again. Bigham did not reply.

Afterwards, Karen felt a surge of satisfaction at having carried out the attack. She had gained revenge and maybe now he would keep away from all children, although she somehow doubted it.

The irony was that this whole sad story might have ended there if it had not been for Archie Bigham's insatiable appetite for children. He had absolutely no control over his urges and as he got older he seemed to feel the need to attack and molest youngsters with ever-increasing regularity. Secretly, he was plotting an even more outrageous crime than that to which he had subjected poor Karen.

. . . .

Karen, now sixteen, sat on the comfortable sofa at home and watched as her mother Terri clasped her hands together nervously. She seemed to have something to say but she was having the utmost difficulty getting it out.

As Terri wrestled with the problem of what to say and how to tell her daughter, Karen already had an inkling about what was about to be revealed. She had suffered so much during her short life that she knew the tell-tale signs in her mother's nervousness.

'There's something I should tell you about your step-dad,' whispered Terri.

Before her mother could explain what she meant, Karen had already guessed the awful truth. She felt sick and faint. She knew that *he* had been committing more horrendous crimes and that *he* had made other young innocents suffer.

'He's done it again, Karen,' explained Terri. 'Only this time to a four-year-old girl.'

Karen felt completely nauseous now. In her mind she could see him doing those horrible things to her when she was eleven. She pictured it happening when she was four and it was too much to contemplate.

There was an awkward silence between mother and daughter. Karen's mind was still filled with appalling images but that silence was like the calm before the storm.

Terri continued, 'It wasn't just the little girl this time. He's raped the mother as well.'

The shadow of that evil monster falling across her bed at night-time leapt into her mind as clearly as if he was there in the room with them. For a few seconds, Karen was an eleven-year-old again, the one who'd hidden under the bed-covers whenever she heard her stepfather's footsteps coming up the stairs at night.

The latest perversion starring Archie Bigham seemed to Karen almost like another victory for child molesters. She felt he was saying, 'I'll never be stopped. I'm going to molest as many children as I can get my hands on.'

At that moment Karen decided she would guarantee that he never got away with it again.

.    .    .

It was July and Karen should have been looking forward to life on a sunny summer's day. She'd just passed eight GCSE exams with flying colours and her future seemed bright.

However, there was a cloud hanging over everything and that cloud was Archie Bigham. She could not get him out of her mind. The evil, sick, perverted monster seemed determined to ruin her entire family. He had to be stopped.

Yet again, the police launched a major investigation into the sexual activities of Bigham. They were dealing with a known paedophile, so the officers were hardly surprised by the new allegations.

On 26 August 1991, Bigham was arrested for assault. At the time he'd been attending a course designed to stop sex offenders from striking again. He was released on bail while investigations continued.

Karen was outraged that Bigham should have been released. It seemed like the final injustice to her. The man who had abused and terrorised her and then committed even worse crimes with a mother and a four-year-old was being allowed to walk free yet again. To rub salt into the wounds of her fury, he had been released on bail pending an eventual trial. Nobody seemed prepared to put this monster behind bars.

Karen was a ball of knotted-up tension by this stage. She was desperate to pour her feelings out to someone and began confiding in a friend, twenty-seven-year-old Vince Scott. He had met her at a burger bar on the Southend seafront where she worked in a summer job.

As holidaymakers swarmed in and out of the restaurant, Karen and Vince discussed how to remedy the situation with Bigham. Vince was just as outraged as Karen when she told him the story. After he had heard it all, Karen got down to brass tacks.

'Will you sort it out?'

Vince did not hesitate in his reply. 'I'll do him.'

'I want him done good. It doesn't matter if he ends up in a pine box.'

With those words, Archie Bigham's fate was sealed. Although Karen had never truly intended to murder the pervert, she undoubtedly wanted him to suffer.

Within days, Karen's older brother Paul was also recruited into the team to 'get' Bigham.

The plan was to give the paedophile a good beating and make him suffer the way he made so many others suffer. He was going to get a taste of his own medicine.

On Bank Holiday Monday, 31 August 1992, Bigham went to his local pub. While he was out, Vince and Paul broke into the pervert's home in Barking. Vince handed Paul a knife and they sat and waited for Bigham to return.

The paedophile finally stumbled into the house in the early hours, completely unaware of his visitors. The two men caught him totally by surprise, grabbed him and forced him to sit at a table so that they could begin their interrogation.

'Why do you do it? What sexual satisfaction do you get out of abusing kids?' said Vince, his voice quivering with anger and disgust.

Archie did not reply. He could not, not without incriminating himself further. He just sat in silence, waiting for the next move.

Meanwhile Paul was working himself into a terrible rage. Not only did he keep thinking about the sexual abuse that man had committed on his innocent young sister but he also kept remembering all the physical abuse he had taken from Bigham.

Paul began repeatedly stabbing the wooden table right in front of the convicted pervert. Bigham sweated as he watched.

'I'm going to kill you! I'm going to kill you! I'm going to kill you!'

Bigham looked terrified. He knew he had to say something, otherwise his fate would be sealed. Slowly, he mumbled little titbits of information. The two men made him speak more clearly. It was then that Bigham admitted inflicting all those beatings on Paul. He confessed to sexually abusing Karen and those other relatives. Archie

Bigham was battling for his life. He was admitting his most heinous crimes in exchange for survival ... or so he hoped.

However, providing the sordid details of his most recent molestation simply incited his assailants. Vince exploded, grabbed the knife from Paul and stabbed Bigham viciously. Paul got the weapon back from his pal and followed suit almost immediately. They were like two hungry dogs baying for blood, taking it in turn to wield the one knife and plunge it into his body.

Bleeding badly, Archie tried to make a run for it but Paul and Vince were not going to let him off that lightly. They pulled him back and each took it in turn to stab him in the body, as deeply and painfully as possible.

The attack was becoming almost unreal in their minds but they could not stop themselves. They had lost control. The figure before them represented the lowest of the low. They felt no remorse. They just wanted revenge. This animal needed to be punished. They did not stop until he was dead.

Afterwards both men felt immensely satisfied. It was a good job well done. They had rid the world of a truly evil person and the rest of society should be grateful to them. Certainly, they had not intended actually to kill him, it just happened that way. In any case, Bigham was better off dead as far as they were concerned. Of course, the police did not see it quite like that.

Within days of detectives launching a murder hunt, they began to suspect that Karen was involved. Bigham's arrest record clearly related the assault on her, for which he had been prosecuted. Investigators started questioning her and people who knew her. It wasn't long before she was arrested. The police were sympathetic but she couldn't be allowed to get away with murder.

In March 1994, Karen, her brother Paul, Vince Scott and a friend called Gary Lee – who had disposed of the knife used to kill Bigham – appeared at the Old Bailey in London.

Karen, now aged eighteen and the mother of a nine-month-old baby, told the jury she didn't order her step-father's death but had just wanted him beaten up.

'I blame myself because of the conversation I had with Vincent,' she confessed. 'I never told him to kill him. I told him I was upset that my stepfather had done it again.'

Karen denied aiding and abetting murder, and Vince Scott and Paul Bigham denied murder.

The jury accepted that none of the defendants had set out to murder Archie Bigham. Paul, now nineteen, was convicted of manslaughter and jailed for three and a half years. Vince was also convicted of manslaughter but was jailed for five years. Both were cleared of murder. Gary Lee was cleared of aiding and abetting murder and manslaughter and was placed on probation for two years after admitting disposing of the knife used to kill Archie.

Karen was led sobbing from the dock after being found guilty of aiding and abetting the manslaughter of her step-father. She was jailed for a year.

During the hearing, prosecuting counsel David Spens told the court: 'In her eyes, the court which had put Archibald Bigham on probation had failed to stop him from doing it again.'

# 9

*'Since women do most delight in revenge, it may seem but feminine manhood to be vindictive.'*

**Sir Thomas Browne, *Christian Morals* (1716)**

# A SORT OF FEMME FATALE

Their eyes first met across a crowded ice-skating rink. She was just fifteen, tall, shapely and very confident. He was seventeen, awkward, shy and extremely inexperienced.

Andrew Morgan watched Jacqueline gliding gracefully over the ice and told a friend she was the prettiest girl he had ever seen. As their eyes locked for a second time, she performed a twirl on the rink just for him. He looked in wonderment at her long, slender legs and well-proportioned body.

Jacqueline had also noticed Andrew immediately and she liked what she saw. She might have been a schoolgirl but she had the instincts of a woman and she knew full well when a boy was interested in her and responded accordingly.

*Jacqueline Morgan, jailed for two years for the grevious bodily harm of her husband.*

Without any hesitation, she glided over to the side of the rink where Andrew was leaning and they struck up a conversation. Andrew was almost too excited to speak. He could not quite believe that this glamorous figure was actually talking to him. They swapped pleasantries at first. What school do you go to? Who are your friends? That sort of thing.

Throughout this, Andrew was aware that she was sizing him up for romance. Her eyes kept panning up and down his body. It should have been the other way round but that was typical of Jacqueline. She had been pretty spoilt at home in south Wales. The only girl in a small family, she got what she wanted and knew full well how to manipulate people for her own advantage.

Andrew was the complete opposite. His mind was firmly focused on starting his own business one day and making a success of his life, almost to the exclusion of other, more social pleasures. Later he openly admitted he was completely swept off his feet by Jacqueline.

Neither of them did much more skating that day. Instead, they wandered over to the coffee bar inside the ice rink and sat and chatted for what seemed like hours.

That evening, Andrew walked home from the rink on a romantic high. He had never before truly enjoyed the company of a girl. It was strange the way that just talking to Jacqueline had made him feel so happy.

After that first meeting, Andrew spent days trying to engineer a way to bump into Jacqueline again. He could not get her out of his mind. In the daytime he walked around in a virtual trance and at night he found it difficult to sleep. The only solution was to find her and ask her out properly.

Eventually his dream came true when he literally bumped into Jacqueline near her school in Cardiff. Andrew was the happiest man in the world when he spotted her and he immediately picked up where they had left off at the ice rink.

Jacqueline was flattered by Andrew's interest and liked the fact that he was a couple of years older than her. She always found the boys at school a little immature for her liking. Then there was the added bonus that Andrew was starting to make his own living, so he always had more cash to spend than the boys at school. All these factors were important to Jacqueline. She only wanted – and often got – the best. She was used to being treated like a little princess at home, so she expected the same from her boyfriends.

Over the following year, Andrew and Jacqueline dated on a very regular basis. Andrew's infatuation with his young girl-friend developed into a full-blown romance and they enjoyed going to the cinema, eating out and sometimes making love.

When Jacqueline announced she was leaving school, Andrew did not hesitate to suggest they should move in together. He could think of nothing better than waking up with his beautiful girlfriend beside him every morning. He would be the envy of his friends because they were always reminding him what a good catch he had made in Jacqueline.

So, just before her seventeenth birthday, Andrew and Jacqueline moved in together. On the surface it seemed like a match made in heaven. With her stunning blonde hair and bubbly personality, Jacqueline was capable of being a great laugh. She could even drink most of Andrew's friends under the table.

However, there was one aspect of Jacqueline's character that Andrew only discovered after they had moved in together. She had a really nasty temper. The slightest thing would set her off. Something as unimportant as spilling tea on her dress before going off to work would do it and Andrew learnt to shrink into the background whenever she had such tantrums.

One time, Jacqueline flipped out about a girl who she claimed was eyeing Andrew up when they went out to the pub with some pals. Andrew had noticed how Jacqueline became really quiet about halfway through the evening but thought nothing of it until they got home. Then she had gone completely crazy with him, shouting and swearing about 'that bitch' and how she had spotted Andrew smiling back at the other girl.

Andrew was bemused and slightly disturbed by Jacqueline's outburst and told her not to be so ridiculous, but that just made Jacqueline worse. She continued ranting and raving at him and then made an extraordinary admission.

'I've hit girls before and if she comes near you I'll get her.'

Andrew sat in stunned silence for a few moments, trying to digest what his lover was saying. Then Jacqueline proudly elaborated. It transpired that she had once broken a girl's jaw at school when that girl dared to flirt with one of her boyfriends before Andrew. Jacqueline then went on to reveal that there had been other times, too. In fact, she seemed to have made quite a habit of beating people up during her school years.

With a shake of her long, curly, blonde hair she turned towards Andrew as if to say, 'Don't mess with me.' At least that's what Andrew thought many years later, although he then had no inkling of what was eventually going to happen. In his mind, Jacqueline was the girl of his dreams, the girl he loved and adored and the person he wanted to spend the rest of his life with.

For two years the couple lived reasonably happily together. There was the occasional temper tantrum from Jacqueline but they always kissed and made up. Andrew acknowledged that no one was perfect, so putting up with a fiery lady did not seem so bad. In any case, there were other advantages.

Andrew loved being out with Jacqueline because she stood out in a crowd because of her penchant for wonderfully tight-fitting mini-dresses and figure-enhancing stilettos. He knew that most of his friends were still really jealous of the way he had hooked up with such a good-looking girl and Jacqueline revelled in all the attention.

She was particularly pleased with the way that Andrew

had started his own business installing satellite TV systems and was building it up into a highly profitable operation. Her parents had always told her to make sure that the man in her life was a good wage earner, so Andrew fitted the bill perfectly.

Jacqueline accidentally got pregnant two years later but there was no remorse at the news. The couple were financially stable so it would have happened eventually anyway. Andrew was particularly delighted because he thought a child was just what Jacqueline needed. He secretly believed that the responsibility of parenthood might just calm down her vicious temper and that that would be a very good thing indeed.

When a little boy – Rhys – was born, both Andrew and Jacqueline saw him as the final seal on their relationship. Naturally she adored the child and seemed to take to motherhood like a duck to water.

Andrew could not quite believe his good fortune in having such a wonderful girl as Jacqueline as his partner. Now that they had Rhys there was only one more thing to make the perfect picture complete. Both sets of parents had started to remind Andrew and Jacqueline that they really should get married, especially as their relationship seemed so solid. Jacqueline appeared the more reluctant of the two actually to commit to wedlock but Andrew interpreted this as the response of a thoroughly modern woman brought up in the 1990s where a marriage certificate is of no real significance.

Eventually, Jacqueline did bow to parental pressure. When Rhys was three years old, the couple married in a quiet ceremony near their home. Immediately after the wedding, however, things started to change.

Jacqueline became much moodier than she had been previously. She seemed dissatisfied with her life at home looking after Rhys while Andrew worked long hours to keep his business up and running. Then there was that temper of hers. It seemed as if the slightest thing could set her off and once Andrew caught a glimpse of that fury in her sea-blue eyes, it was a danger signal of what was to come. Usually, he would just leave the room or change the subject. There was absolutely no point in prolonging the agony.

In many ways, Andrew tried to bury his head in his work and not worry too much about Jacqueline's mood swings. He just hoped it would all blow over. At home, however, Jacqueline was getting more and more depressed. She talked to her other girlfriends about their lives and discovered they were all going out to nightclubs and having a good time while she was stuck at home with Rhys. Jacqueline was a fun girl at heart and she did not like the fact that other people were having a more enjoyable time than her. Being married made it worse because Jacqueline felt as if there would never be an escape from the drudgery and boredom. She had signed away her rights to freedom and she did not like it one little bit.

·     ·     ·

'I want more freedom. I'm going to move out.'

Andrew couldn't quite believe his ears when Jacqueline announced her plans minutes after he came home from work one night. He never thought it would come to this but, as had always been the case between them, he could not stand in her way. Something stopped him from trying too hard to persuade her not to go. It was a feeling he had. He did not want the marriage to end but he feared that unless she got her wish, something terrible might happen.

On the surface he pleaded with Jacqueline to stay but he knew all along that her mind was made up. She told him she had spoken to her parents and they had agreed to let her and Rhys move in. It was for the best, she explained. Andrew wasn't entirely convinced but Jacqueline always got what Jacqueline wanted.

For the first few months of the split, Andrew and Jacqueline remained on reasonable terms. He would try to see Rhys as often as possible and she was genuinely pleased that his business was going from strength to strength.

The turning point came when Jacqueline heard on the grapevine that Andrew was seeing another girl. The fact that they had separated did not seem to matter to Jacqueline; she was still incensed that he was daring to go out with another woman right under her nose.

Andrew saw it slightly differently. He needed the company of another female and as Jacqueline had been the one who had insisted they separate, what was the harm in it?

When Andrew went to visit Rhys at Jacqueline's parents' home one day, he experienced a full-blown version of that vicious temper of hers. She screamed and yelled at him that she would not stand for him dating other women. He tried to reason with her but by that time she had turned into a wild, crazy, out-of-control personality and he could not handle it so he walked out.

A few days later, Jacqueline commenced divorce proceedings. Andrew was torn between sadness at the break-up of his family and the relief he felt because that temper of Jacqueline's really did worry him.

Then a strange thing happened because Jacqueline became more like her old self again. It was almost as if the divorce proceedings had lifted a veil of insecurity from over her head. She became much more friendly towards Andrew and he became very confused. Only a few weeks earlier his estranged wife had been attacking him like a lunatic. Now she was giving him long lingering kisses every time he popped round to see Rhys.

Behind Jacqueline's charm, however, there was an ulterior motive. She mentioned to Andrew that she wanted him to sell their family house and all their possessions so that she could have her share. Andrew agreed but said that it would have to wait until the divorce was finalised.

The next thing he knew, Jacqueline was on his doorstep with Rhys, announcing that they were moving back in. For a few moments Andrew thought that perhaps they were going to give the marriage another go, but Jacqueline soon put paid to that notion.

Within minutes of arriving at the house she made it very clear to him that she had not come back for any romantic reasons; she simply wanted to stake a claim on the house and their possessions. Andrew finally conceded to friends that night that his marriage was well and truly over.

He soon started getting serious with his new girlfriend and promised himself he would try to end the marriage as cleanly and swiftly as possible so that both of them could get on with the rest of their lives. He also wanted to guarantee that little Rhys was not hurt.

However, having moved back into the house, Jacqueline now wanted Andrew to get out. She shouted and screamed at him on a regular basis, saying that he had no right to be there, but he had no place else to go. Every night it was the same old story. Andrew would come home exhausted from a hard day at work to face a barrage of abuse from his estranged wife. To start with, it was a generalised verbal attack that repeated over and over again that he had to get out. Then Jacqueline became more specific. 'I could have you done over for thirty quid.'

Andrew was staggered when he heard his wife's words. She couldn't possibly mean it, could she?

Then he looked at the cold, steely expression on her face and began to wonder. That night they hardly uttered another word to each other, but the damage had already been done.

A few weeks later, on 22 June 1993, Jacqueline picked up Rhys from a local child minder and arrived home at about five o'clock, almost exactly the same time as Andrew. The couple had agreed to take it in turns to look after their son and the plan that day was for Jacqueline to drop Rhys with Andrew, then go out with a friend and return home by nine that evening so that he could go out.

At about 8.45 p.m., having put Rhys to bed, Andrew had settled into a long comfortable hot bath when he heard Jacqueline come in.

In the hallway, she called out to the couple's dog and then, for some reason, locked him out in the back garden.

Just after that Andrew noticed that everything had gone deathly quiet. He gave it a few moments' thought then got out of the bath, put a towel round his waist and started to have a shave.

Suddenly the door burst open. Andrew just presumed it was Jacqueline or Rhys. Then he turned from the sink to face three men armed with baseball bats and crowbars.

The first man smashed Andrew clean across the face, then dropped his weapon and held him in a head lock. The two other men stood behind him as he yelled at them, 'Smash his right leg, smash his right leg, go for his knee.'

Andrew did not even think about the significance of this remark until later when he realised that they must have known he had a steel plate in his right leg as a result of a serious car crash.

Too stunned even to be frightened, Andrew then suffered a series of hefty blows to the head and body. They were excruciatingly painful but then his body went completely numb, almost as if his entire internal system had shut down. Blood was pouring out of his wounds. Andrew did not even realise that half his skull had caved in as a result of one hefty baseball-bat blow to the side of his head. His brain had literally been punctured by the attackers and his body had basically 'slowed down' as a result.

Then, in the middle of all this, little Rhys woke up and started crying. In the background, Andrew just made out the sound of Jacqueline rushing up the stairs to come to his rescue. She burst into the room and pleaded with the attackers to stop but they took no notice.

The three men kept on smashing into Andrew for at

least another three minutes before he collapsed on the bathroom floor, bloodied and beaten to a pulp. Relieved that it was all over and he was still just alive, Andrew managed to look up as they walked towards the door. One of the men took the crowbar he had used earlier and crashed it down on the left side of Andrew's rib cage. The pain was unbelievable and he kept smashing it down on Andrew over and over again before walking out of the house.

Despite the severe beating, Andrew never stopped worrying about his beloved Rhys and Jacqueline. He feared that they had been attacked by the intruders who had broken into his house and nearly killed him. God knows what they might have done to them.

A next-door neighbour called the emergency services after hearing the explosion of violence and minutes after the men had departed Andrew found himself being rushed to hospital in an ambulance with Jacqueline holding his hand and crying. It was a pitiful, heartbreaking scene.

At the hospital, doctors found that part of Andrew's skull had caved in, both his arms and legs were fractured and his spine and rib cage were seriously damaged. As he lay close to death in intensive care, medics also discovered that the blow to Andrew's head had caused a blood clot on the right side of his brain and he would need surgery to rebuild the right side of his head and face.

That same night, police and forensic experts swarmed all over the Morgan household in a bid to find clues as to the identity of his attackers. Investigators swiftly tracked down a local boy who had seen the three men leaving the house and they identified the ringleader and the second man immediately. They were detained within hours. A warrant was issued for the arrest of the third man, who gave himself up the following day. Two days later, officers arrested Jacqueline on suspicion of being involved and took her to the police station to be questioned.

Back in hospital, Andrew Morgan was clinging to life following the brutal, apparently senseless, attack. Doctors gave strict instructions to his family that under no circumstances was he to be told of Jacqueline's involvement. There were genuine fears that if Andrew was told the truth it might 'send him over the edge'.

Then one of Andrew's friends visited the hospital and let slip to him that Jacqueline had set the whole thing up. Andrew was so shocked by the news that he instantly threw up over the side of the bed. He could not believe it. 'How could she have done that to me?' he kept thinking. How could she have let those thugs walk into their house armed with weapons when their child was sleeping nearby? Andrew knew that things had not exactly being going well between him and Jacqueline, but surely she could not do this?

As Andrew lay in that hospital bed, he started to think back to those little tell-tale signs: the threat to get him beaten up for thirty pounds, the way the dog was locked out while he lay in the bath, the specific attack on his injured right leg. Then the police told him there were no signs of a forced entry, so how else could the men have got in?

A week after the attack, doctors decided it was safe to operate on Andrew. During ten hours of surgery they cut him from ear to ear over the top of his head, peeled back his face and inserted metal plates with nuts and bolts around his cheek, eye socket and skull.

By the time he was released from hospital, Jacqueline and the other men had been charged with wounding with intent to cause grievous bodily harm. Andrew took Rhys to live with his parents.

His life was destroyed. Before the attack he had a thriving business but now that had to be closed down. The following months were dreadful. Andrew could not sleep because he was so terrified he wouldn't wake up and when he did fall asleep he was plagued by horrendous nightmares.

At Cardiff Crown Court in January 1994, all three men admitted grievous bodily harm, but twenty-four-year-old Jacqueline denied the charge. In court she said she never intended Andrew to be harmed – just frightened.

The jury took just forty minutes to find her guilty but they convicted on a lesser count (which means no specific intent to injure was involved) because they couldn't prove she intended to hurt her husband so badly.

Andrew Morgan is trying to start his life again, but he is not fully recovered. When they caved in his skull, the bones crushed tendons in his eyes so he still has double vision and is due for further surgery. If that does not work, doctors have warned him to expect to suffer for the rest of his life.

'Jacqueline might look as pretty as a Barbie doll, but at the end of the day she's vicious. And I think that's the way she'll always be,' he said after the case.

# 10

'Sweet is revenge
— especially to women.'

*Byron, Don Juan (1819–24)*

# INFLAMED
# EMOTIONS

The deep orange, early-morning light bathed the entire San Fernando Valley in gentle warmth. Hummingbirds hovered silently as they homed in on the bird-of-paradise plants that provide them with a tasty breakfast. Overhead, the constant high-pitched tone of single-engined light aircraft sweeping through the skies was a noisy reminder of the metropolis of Los Angeles which lay just twenty miles to the south.

August 12 1993 was a scorchingly hot day in the San Fernando Valley. As temperatures nudged into the low hundreds, a hazy film of smog hung over the vast basin that is one of the largest suburban developments in California.

Right in the centre of the valley lies the much-varied city of Van Nuys. Split in two by the valley's busiest airport, Van Nuys is a mish-mash of comfortable, detached, single-storey homes in the south, and scruffy, tightly-built apartment blocks in the north, some of which have become breeding grounds for many of southern California's most notorious street gangs.

Most weeks, police find themselves examining the corpses of at least one victim of a gangland shoot-out. It is a dog-eat-dog world where life is as cheap as the fifty dollars it costs to buy a revolver. Petty crime thrives on the streets of northern Van Nuys, encouraged by the hot weather that exists most of the year and the American social divide.

Not surprisingly, the divorce rate in the area is well over fifty per cent and that means that the Van Nuys Superior Court tends to be a very busy place most days. Couples seeking to end their marriages often arrive at the yellow, sixties-built courthouse as early as eight o'clock so as to be first in line for a hearing.

So it was on this August day when yet another divorce action was initiated at the court in Van Nuys. This time, however, rather than just breaking up a family, it was to end in even more tragic circumstances.

After fifteen years together, Pamela and Kenneth Lisi had already filed for a petition to end their marriage but they still had to decide who would get custody of their two young daughters, aged four and eleven. They had tried to do it the civilised way over the previous ten months, but it just had not worked out. Now they had to ask a judge to make the decision for them. The Lisi situation was very tragic, even when compared to the other divorce actions being heard that day.

Behind the polite façade that existed between Pam and

Ken as their eyes met outside the court that morning, lay a seething hatred and a whole series of very damaging allegations, plus the fact that Pam was suffering from a dreadful, debilitating illness.

There were also Pam's relatives. They were incensed that Ken even had the nerve to try to gain sole custody of the children, considering the gravity of their mother's illness. How could he be so cold-hearted about her circumstances? How could he deliberately set out to part a dying mother from her own children?

Pam's mother, seventy-three-year-old Jo Lula Haynes, knew what it was like to bring up children single-handed. She had done precisely that with Pam and her brothers and sisters and she wasn't about to stand back and see her daughter's children taken away from her.

Since Pam's illness, Jo Lula had become her daughter's steadfast support, the one she turned to for help, love and guidance. Jo Lula – who had lived with Pamela since her marriage had broken up – had become like a second mother to those little girls.

No one knows if it was in desperation to prevent Pam from losing her children or whether something really had happened, but Jo Lula and her daughter made sworn statements before the hearing, claiming that Ken Lisi had sexually abused one of their daughters.

They alleged that Lisi continually molested the four-year-old in a series of horrific attacks which had occurred during the previous few months. If true, the claims were proof enough that Lisi should never be allowed to get his hands on those children ever again.

Ken Lisi said he was outraged by the claims and insisted they were part of a campaign by Pam's family to prevent him from getting custody of his daughters. Lisi even paid for one of the state's top child psychologists to examine his youngest daughter to find out if there was any evidence to support the claims. The psychologist reported to the court that day that there was absolutely no proof of sexual molestation.

Ken Lisi felt completely vindicated and he was determined to push ahead for complete custody of the children. However, he did not help things by becoming very angry in the court and showing verbal hostility towards his wife's camp. He frequently screamed and shouted at the judge and beat his fists on the table in court. He also mocked his wife's relatives, especially his mother-in-law Jo Lula. He believed that she had orchestrated the 'sex slur' campaign against him.

Jo Lula believed that Ken's attitude was yet more evidence of his unstable character and precisely the reason why he should not be given any right of custody of the two girls. So Lula watched his manic behaviour from across the Van Nuys courtroom that day and convinced herself that this man was evil. She had no doubt that the sexual molestation allegations were true despite what that doctor had said.

Superior Court judge Robert M. Letteau listened to all the evidence in court that morning and was astounded by the wild accusations coming from both camps. Even he was unused to such intense hatred between two parties in a divorce action.

Letteau was even more surprised when Pam's lawyer

revealed that her client was suffering from the seriously debilitating illness of lupus, a degenerative, ulcerating skin disease which required 'significant medication'. Everyone in the court felt immensely sorry for Pam Lisi at that point. Her mother, Jo Lula, was so upset that she wept quietly.

When Letteau inquired as to how Pam could look after two children when suffering from such a serious illness, it was immediately pointed out that she had the back-up of her mother and a number of other relatives. The judge did not pass comment but simply noted that fact on his notepad.

Across the courtroom, Jo Lula prayed that her daughter would be granted sole custody. She had long since fallen out with Ken Lisi and could not bear the thought of ever having to meet that 'animal' again. She had told her daughter that she was well rid of him and she hoped this would be the last time they ever had to be in the same room together.

When the judge retired to consider his verdict on the question of custody, Pam looked to her mother for support. Jo Lula gave her a thumbs-up sign because she could not believe that any judge would refuse her daughter permission to live out the remainder of her life with her children.

A few minutes later Judge Letteau reappeared and solemnly declared that Ken Lisi should gain sole custody because he feared that Pam Lisi was relying too heavily on her relatives to look after the girls.

Pam and her relatives sat back in stunned silence. Then Jo Lula started shouting in the judge's direction but was silenced by a clerk. Pam's attorney shrugged his shoulders and said 'sorry' but there was nothing he could do about it. The judge's decision was final.

For Jo Lula Haynes it was the worst day of her life and there is little doubt that her daughter felt just as heart-broken.

Ken Lisi's life was, by all accounts, fairly normal, apart from the claims of child sex abuse that were made against him by Pam's family. Following the break-up of their marriage the previous November, he had moved to the town of Lancaster, some eighty miles north east of Los Angeles, where his parents lived. Ken genuinely believed that he could make a good home there for his daughters.

Pam's illness undoubtedly made the divorce action far more emotive than it might otherwise have been but, as Ken pointed out to his friends and family, it was not his fault that Pam had got sick and however much he felt sorry for her it would not help to mend their broken marriage.

Ken had been working for many years as a producer of music and voice casting for projects in Walt Disney theme parks across the world. His colleagues at his office just down the road from Van Nuys always found him a very polite and mild-mannered guy. Nothing was too much trouble for Ken. It all seemed in sharp contrast to the impression he had given to his in-laws.

The accusations of child molestation were constantly simmering in the thoughts of Pam's mother and other relatives, causing frequent, unsavoury flare-ups between Ken Lisi and his wife's family.

· · ·

The end of October 1993 was marked by Hallowe'en, a billion-dollar-a-year business in California. Each year, on the last day of October, the entire nation becomes obsessed by dead bodies, vampires and witches. Children are swept up by the scenario and some houses are decorated like something out of Hansel and Gretel.

The Hallowe'en tradition had been sparked off three hundred years previously by a group of devil worshippers in Salem, Massachusetts who had decided to kill some witches.

However, back on that October evening in 1993, children done up in ghoulish fancy dress, often splattered with fake blood, were patrolling the neat and tidy streets of the suburb of Northridge, trick or treating for sweets from their neighbours.

So it was that Ken Lisi found himself driving through Northridge towards his estranged wife's home where he intended to pick up their two daughters, following a weekend at their mother's house. After the acrimony at that August court hearing, Ken and Pam had somehow come to a mutual 'understanding' and Ken had allowed the girls to visit their mother occasionally, despite the sole-custody order imposed by the judge. After all, reasoned Ken, he could not keep them away from their mother when she was so seriously ill.

Trailing him that night were Ken's elderly parents, Ernest Lisi and his wife, who intended to follow their son home to Lancaster following a day out in Los Angeles.

As Ken pulled up outside the house in Louise Avenue, which his wife shared with her mother Jo Lula, he wondered what kind of spirits the children would be in after spending the weekend with their sick mother. He hoped they would be in a happy mood as they had a long drive back to Lancaster that evening.

Ken rang the door bell at 7.20 p.m., waved at his father waiting across the street and wondered why it seemed so quiet in the house. Usually the girls came rushing out to greet him. He pressed the bell again. Suddenly the door was swung open by the one person Ken dreaded having to meet, his mother-in-law Jo Lula.

As she stood in the doorway, Ken did not notice the .38 calibre revolver in her right hand.

'Are the kids here?'

Jo Lula said nothing at first. She had a strange, demonic look in her eyes. But Ken was more than used to his mother-in-law's eccentric behaviour. He did not think twice about it.

'Are they here?'

'The kids aren't here and nor is Pam …' She hesitated. Ken was starting to get really pissed off.

'What the …'

'You're not going to see the kids again,' she interrupted. Then she thought to herself, 'This is for them.' She raised the gun, pulled the trigger and shot Ken Lisi in the leg.

He fell to the ground clutching his leg. By lying there in front of her, however, he simply provided an easier target for her to aim at. Now she had his entire body clear in her sights.

Across the street, Ernest Lisi had seen his son fall with his own eyes. It had seemed almost unreal, like something out of a cops-and-robbers TV show. But it was real enough.

Ernest scrambled out of his car and headed towards the house as fast as he could but there was no stopping Jo Lula.

BANG! She thought of those child sex charges alleged against him.

BANG! She thought of her seriously ill daughter deprived of the chance to live with her children during her dying days.

BANG! She thought of the mental cruelty Ken put her daughter through before they separated.

By the time Jo Lula had finished, Ken lay writhing on the ground with numerous gaping holes in his upper chest.

At that moment, Ernest Lisi arrived with his wife and they managed to subdue and disarm seventy-three-year-old Jo Lula with relative ease. She was proud of her 'achievement' and had no need to run. She wanted the world to know what she had done for her dying daughter – Pamela and her daughters were not even at home at the time.

Lisi was rushed to the nearby Northridge Medical Center by paramedics but died a short while after the shooting.

Ernest Lisi could not quite believe what had happened. He had known that his son's divorce battle was a bitter affair but never in his wildest dreams had he imagined it would end up like this.

'It was very tragic,' said a heartbroken Ernest Lisi shortly after the shooting. 'I have no idea why it happened. I haven't the slightest idea why she did what she did.'

Los Angeles police arrested Jo Lula Haynes and booked her for murder. She was ordered to be held without bail in Van Nuys Jail pending an arraignment. Her trial is expected to be heard sometime in 1995.

Police homicide detective Rick Swanston, of the Los Angeles Police Department's West Valley section, said: 'She just opened fire on him. In domestic matters, child-custody matters, emotions become inflamed. People do violent things.'

Shortly after the shooting, Superior Court Judge Robert M. Letteau – the same official who gave Ken Lisi custody of his children – ordered police to pick up the two girls and deliver them to county social workers until a suitable family member could be found to care for them. He said it would be detrimental to the children's welfare for them to stay in their mother's care. He did not acknowledge that his earlier decision on their parental custody might have contributed to the tragedy.

Suzanne Harris, who represented Pamela Lisi in the divorce case, said that Jo Lula Haynes had never shown any indications of violence. 'She is a very nice older lady; a very gentle lady. A little odd-looking with some funny manner-isms, but she's the gentlest person I ever met.'

Meanwhile Ken Lisi's father Ernest added: 'Ken's problems are over now. The police have her in custody and will do with her what they will …'

# 11

'Revenge is a much more punctual
paymaster than gratitude.'

Charles Caleb Colton, *Lacon* (1825)

# THE BORED
# NYMPHO

Rebecca Smith wrapped her arms around her sturdily-built lover and stroked the hairs on his chest. Then, with a sudden snake-like movement she snapped a hair out. He winced with pain, then saw the smile on her face and laughed. Rebecca did love to play games. She also loved to inflict a brief amount of pain on all around her – and that included her workman lover Thad.

Rebecca needed to be in control the whole time. The mother of three grown boys, she enjoyed the power to do whatever she wanted with Thad. Their passionate affair had reignited after a break of almost twenty years. The second time around, Thad later recalled, the love making was even less inhibited.

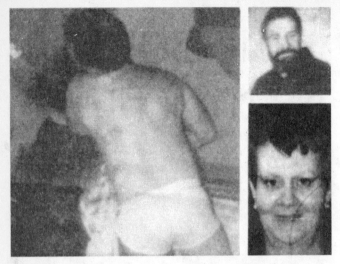

Top left: *The body of Harold Smith found sprawled in a pool of blood in his trailer.*

Top right: *Harold Smith.*

Bottom right: *Rebecca Smith, who ordered her lover to help murder her husband.*

Thad had first met Rebecca when she was married to the father of her three sons. She had told Thad that her husband was in the habit of beating her up. Within days of meeting, she lured him to her home on some pretext or other one afternoon and when she opened the front door with a silky dressing gown on, Thad knew they would end up in bed together.

That affair only lasted two months and mainly revolved around Rebecca's ability to enjoy sex in just about any place she happened to be at the moment the urge came upon her. Thad – then a young, impressionable teenager – was completely swept off his feet. She taught him things he never even knew existed.

Thad was heartbroken when Rebecca told him she was ending the relationship because she was moving out of state. Thad always reckoned that his disappointment about Rebecca's 'desertion' led him to marry and divorce four times before they met again.

In 1986, Thad ran into Rebecca in his local store in Laurinberg, North Carolina. She might have been twenty years older but she still cut a fine figure.

Rebecca was immediately entranced by Thad. He looked as magnificent as ever as she panned her eyes up and down his body while he stood there, slightly awkwardly talking to her. She decided there and then that she was going to have him again.

Just a few weeks later the affair restarted. The love making was so wild and uninhibited that it was like starting a completely new relationship. As usual, Rebecca did most of the running. She would appear at Thad's little house on the edge of town whenever the moment took her fancy and Thad never failed to oblige. After those four disastrous marriages, this was the ideal relationship. He needed sex but the last thing he required was a full-time woman.

However, Thad soon began to discover that Rebecca's insatiable appetite for sex had developed in a quite unusual way since their earlier liaison. In fact, he started to wonder whether she wasn't just a little sick in the head because she did not seem to be able to enjoy traditional love making any more. There always had to be some dangerous edge to it.

Thad never forgot the time Rebecca showed up at his house with her son Brian, then in his early twenties, and

Brian's pretty young girlfriend. Thad was a little surprised as Rebecca usually demanded sex within minutes of arriving at Thad's house and he did not exactly expect her to bring guests, especially her own son.

The foursome enjoyed a few beers and some bourbon together and then, as her son and his girlfriend sat in the sitting room of the house, Rebecca stripped down to her stockings, bra and panties and did a little dance for her guests.

Both Brian and his girlfriend applauded and tried to encourage Rebecca to strip off completely. She did not need that much encouragement. Thad sat transfixed by the entire episode, unsure whether to applaud along with the others or to try to put a stop to the proceedings.

A few minutes later, Rebecca declared she was going to liven up the action even further. She told a stunned Thad that she wanted to go to the bedroom with him to have sex. Naturally, he obliged, although he couldn't help being a bit surprised that she talked that way in front of her own son.

Thad did not notice Rebecca winking at her son as she got up. A moment later she grabbed Thad's hand and pulled him towards the only bedroom in the house. Brian did the same with his girlfriend and followed his mother and her lover.

In the bedroom, Thad found himself even more confused. Rebecca calmly explained to her lover that she wanted her son to take photographs of them having sex. She said it almost as plainly as a mother might explain to her child that he should do his homework, although in this case it was obvious that Brian did not need teaching.

Brian's girlfriend giggled and then gave Brian the camera. Rebecca ripped open Thad's trousers and within minutes the flashbulb was popping over and over again ...

By the end of that evening, Thad felt rather differently about Rebecca. It was all very well enjoying outrageous sex in all sorts of weird and wonderful places but he did find it a bit strange to be performing in front of her son. It made him feel kind of uneasy.

When, a few weeks later, Rebecca added another unusual dimension to her illicit affair with Thad, he decided it was time to end the relationship.

The final straw came as Rebecca prepared to strip off for more sex as she sat on Thad's couch one afternoon. About to unhook her bra, she paused momentarily. 'Would you do me a big favour if I paid you five thousand dollars?' she asked, very matter-of-factly.

'What you want me to do for that kind of money?' replied a puzzled Thad.

'Kill Harold.'

There was a long silence as Thad considered why she should be asking him to kill her long-suffering husband Harold. The sex scene with her son had been weird enough but now the alarm bells were ringing continuously in his head.

'I don't go round killing people, Rebecca. It ain't right.'

'Oh well,' sighed Rebecca, still managing to make the entire conversation sound less important than if she was haggling over the price of a bag of apples at the local grocery store. 'Maybe you know someone else who'd do it.'

Thad was starting to get really uncomfortable now. 'Hell no. Just drop it, Rebecca.'

Rebecca finally got the message and changed the subject but Thad knew it was only a matter of time before she found herself an assassin.

·  ·  ·

Billy Ray McGee was the perfect replacement lover for Rebecca Smith after she and Thad finished their fling. Billy Ray was a fitness fanatic who'd become obsessed with weight training after a few stints in jail for thieving.

No one ever questioned Rebecca's motives in hooking up with Billy Ray. It was just taken for granted that she required abnormally large amounts of bedtime activity and that her husband Harold could never, in a month of Sundays, provide his wife with what she seemed to crave every moment of the day.

Harold was a quietly-spoken, shy type of guy. At the plant where he worked incredibly hard, he was well liked and renowned for working through lunch breaks and volunteering to do endless overtime.

Harold was so devoted to Rebecca that he even routinely handed over his entire pay packet to his wife, who gave him back thirty dollars a week spending money. He never once complained. He just wanted to ensure that she was constantly happy.

On 15 July 1989, Harold excitedly told his work colleagues that he was looking forward to leaving his routine world for a fishing trip. Fishing was a pleasure Harold usually enjoyed with his three stepsons. On this occasion,

however, he was going alone because all of the boys –
Rebecca's children by her previous marriage – were
employed full time and could not get any time off to
join him.

'He was so happy,' explained one co-worker at the plant.
'All he talked about was going to the beach and catching
twenty-three fish at a time.'

Harold had worked at the Corning plant since 1973 and
had built his earnings up to a very impressive twenty-two
thousand dollars a year, considerably more than his base
salary because he was so willing to work overtime.

Since his marriage to Rebecca more than fifteen years
earlier, Harold had always got on very well with his three
stepsons and, besides fishing trips, they often went on
vacations in the mountains and lakes nearby. Harold had,
according to relatives, 'raised those boys as if they were his
own flesh and blood'.

On the face of it, Harold's marriage to Rebecca seemed
perfectly normal but, inevitably, he began to hear some of
the rumours about his wife's recreational habits and even
confessed to one colleague at work that everything was not
going so well on the domestic front.

However, Harold had insisted that he would sort out
his 'problems' in his own careful way. Undoubtedly, he
knew that those 'problems' had been caused by his wife's
interest in other, younger men. Whether he actually chose
never to confront his wife about her addiction to sex no one
knows, but he certainly did not want to face up to the facts.

There was another very strange aspect to his marriage
which was not so apparent – Rebecca's obsession with black

magic. In early 1989, Rebecca started visiting a local woman who claimed to be a witch capable of casting spells and putting hexes on people. Rebecca was particularly interested in cursing her husband's life. She complained bitterly that Harold was no fun and that she was completely bored by her life as Mrs Smith.

Still, none of this was going to ruin Harold's plans for a quiet fishing trip where he could escape all the pressures of life and just worry about how many nibbles he was going to get on the end of his line.

On Friday, 13 July 1989, Harold set off in his blue Chevrolet truck for the two-hour drive to the family's holiday trailer at Cherry Grove, a beautiful strip of coastline on South Carolina's Grand Strand, which stretches some forty miles between Georgetown and Little River.

On that Sunday (15 July), with Harold safely packed off on his getaway break at the trailer, Rebecca Smith enjoyed an afternoon of love making with Billy Ray before he took a nap. She awoke him early that evening and they smoked a cannabis joint and snorted cocaine before she announced that she wanted to take her son Brian Locklear to the beach so that he could go fishing with Harold.

Accompanying Rebecca and Brian on the drive were Billy Ray McGee and a relative, Charles Gainey. The four of them took the car of another of Rebecca's sons who was working at the time. Brian drove and the foursome got a little spooked when they hit a wild animal on the road to the beach.

'I knew something bad was going to happen after that,' explained Gainey later.

When the foursome arrived at the beach area, they stopped for a short time at a picturesque fishing pier to admire the sunset and then drove to the mobile-home park where the Smith family trailer was located.

Gainey was puzzled when Rebecca barked orders at her son to dim the car lights as he drove towards the trailer, and then she instructed him not to park near the actual trailer.

'You and Billy lie down on the floor. I don't want Harold knowing I got a lot of company,' muttered Rebecca coldly. They did as they were told.

Moments later Rebecca and her beloved son disappeared in the direction of the trailer. Suddenly, a light came on in the trailer and they watched as Harold came to the door to let them in. Gainey stayed out of view but later claimed he was puzzled by the fact that Rebecca was hiding a baseball bat behind her back at the moment her husband opened the door.

For a few more minutes Gainey and Billy Ray remained hidden in the back of the car. Then Brian appeared and ordered them to go back to the pier and get some soft drinks. Gainey and Billy Ray returned within ten minutes to be greeted by an excited Rebecca, who rushed to the car and said, 'I did it. I did it. He's dead.'

All three of them entered the trailer. Gainey was ordered to go down the hall and 'look at what Becky had done'. Harold was lying half out of bed, half on the floor, making gurgling noises. Just at that moment, one of the men – they disputed who in later testimony – took the baseball bat off a counter and smashed Harold in the head again 'to finish him off'.

Then Gainey watched in astonishment as Brian Locklear grabbed some hand lotion from a nearby cupboard and smothered it all over his dead stepfather's fingers so that he could remove a horseshoe-shaped ring. Meanwhile, a cool-as-ice Rebecca Smith was moving around the trailer wiping things down with a cloth so that there would no fingerprints on display when the police arrived at the scene.

As they were leaving, McGee – the only professional criminal among them – smashed the flimsy door to the trailer with the baseball bat just to ensure that the entire incident looked as if it had happened following a break-in.

During the drive home they pulled the car up on a bridge and Rebecca's son Brian tossed the bloodied baseball bat into the river.

After returning to the family home in Laurinberg a few hours later, Rebecca ordered Brian to take the horseshoe ring to the witch doctor she had previously visited. She told him it was 'payment' for her previous efforts to kill Harold by means of witchcraft before she decided upon a more traditional approach.

After visiting the witch doctor, Brian returned to the family home to fetch a pair of Harold's trousers. They put these in a cake pan along with some sulphur and red onions, then burned the whole lot. The witch doctor had assured them that this would prevent the police from tracking down Rebecca and her fellow killers.

With the killing completed, Rebecca decided that the next stage of her plan should be put into operation.

'You gotta help. It's my husband. I'm real worried about him.' Rebecca Smith sounded very concerned about her husband's whereabouts when she called the North Myrtle Beach police department in South Carolina. She told the operator she had been unable to get her husband on the phone despite repeated attempts. She was afraid something might have happened to him.

Communications technician Dot Sorra assured her that just as soon as the police information computer network was programmed, the information would be acted upon.

Patrolman Asa Bailey took the call from a dispatcher and headed up to the trailer park at Cherry Grove. At first he got no answer after knocking on the door. He walked around and peered through the windows, but everything seemed okay.

Then he got round to the back door. Again, there was no answer but still nothing seemed amiss. Back at the front door a few minutes later, Bailey noticed the doorknob was scraped and dented with what appeared to be pry marks. He tried the door properly this time. It was unlocked.

Bailey opened the door tentatively, then called out as he walked into the trailer's small living area. Next to it was a clean, compact kitchen with hardly an item out of place. Bailey stood and considered the scene for a few moments. It someone had battered and smashed their way in, surely things would be in a more chaotic state?

Then Bailey walked down the narrow hallway towards the only bedroom on the left. He glanced through the door and did a double take. Lying half on and half off a blood-stained bed was the body of a man dressed only in underpants. Bailey could only see the back of the dead man's head, lying in a large bloody stain on the carpet.

After rapidly searching the rest of the mobile home in case anyone else was present, Bailey returned to his police cruiser and made an urgent request for a supervisor and a detective.

Shortly after 2 p.m., Chief of Detectives Walt Floyd and Detective Don Repec were making a detailed inspection of the crime scene. At first they could not even find anything to provide identification of the victim although there were many bloodstains in the bedroom. Large quantities also blotted the bedclothing and the floor under the victim's head. Blood was also splattered over the wall and even on the shade of the bedside lamp. Floyd and Repec immediately deduced that the drops of blood must have been shed in the backswing of a bloody weapon.

Detective Repec painstakingly photographed every angle of the death scene with a video camera as his colleagues began their meticulous search of the premises.

It was only when the victim's body was moved and turned over that it became obvious just how horrific a beating had been inflicted on Harold Smith. The battering had been so severe that one eye socket had been crushed and the eyeball itself knocked out of the victim's head.

Both detectives were concerned by the lack of evidence of any furniture or belongings being disturbed and they rapidly established that the entire trailer had been cleaned of fingerprints. The North Myrtle Beach police force had not dealt with a murder inquiry for four years so this investigation was getting the full treatment.

A few hours into their inquiries, one of the investigators discovered that someone had used the toilet in the trailor but had not flushed it. Probers took samples of the urine still in the toilet bowl and, a few days later, it was determined that the sample contained cocaine residue. The victim had no known involvement with drugs and there was no evidence of drug taking in his body.

The discovery of that cocaine convinced the two detectives that they were dealing with something much more complex than a straightforward burglary that had turned to violence. They rapidly established that Rebecca Smith had a vast sexual appetite and some of her conquests began, as they sometimes say, to sing like canaries.

On 8 August 1989, Rebecca Smith and Billy Ray McGee were arrested and charged with the murder of Harold Dean Smith. Her relative, Charles Gainey, was charged as an accessory, as was Brian Locklear, despite the damning evidence against him.

With information provided by Gainey, lawmen located a baseball bat that had been tossed off a bridge over the nearby Waccamaw River. The State Law Enforcement Division (SLED) analysts detected bloodstains on the object. They also discovered, embedded on the bat's grain, paint that was later matched to paint on the door at the murder scene.

Shortly after her arrest, Rebecca Smith made a statement to police in which she blamed Billy Ray McGee for the murder of her husband. She claimed that he was the one who actually smashed her husband to death with that baseball bat.

Then her loyal son Brian also claimed that McGee was the actual killer. Meanwhile McGee claimed that Rebecca

Smith had persuaded him to help her with the killing after she regularly visited him in jail during an earlier sentence, each time bringing his spending money in amounts of $15 to $30. Rebecca even bought cocaine through McGee on his release and he accompanied her on at least twenty visits to a witch doctor whom Smith wanted to put a death spell on her husband.

In early 1990, all four suspects – Billy McGee, Rebecca Smith, Charles Gainey and Brian Locklear – were indicted on various charges in connection with the murder of Harold Smith.

In December 1990, almost eighteen months after her husband's murder, Rebecca Smith went on trial for her life in the Horry County Courthouse in Conway. The other three had already entered pleas in connection with the case.

The jury deliberated for nine hours before returning a guilty verdict and Rebecca Smith was sentenced to die in the electric chair. However, the case was appealed and at a retrial in February 1994, Rebecca Smith was again found guilty of first-degree murder but the jury declined to give her the death penalty. She was sentenced to life imprisonment and is currently serving her term in the South Carolina correction system. The new trial was further complicated by fresh claims from her son Brian that he was the one who had beaten and killed Harold Smith. This evidence was discounted after the court was told that Brian Locklear was a self-confessed bisexual who had tested HIV-positive.

Meanwhile, Billy McGee and Brian Locklear were sentenced to thirty-five-year jail terms and Gainey got fifteen years, but was released on parole after helping authorities with evidence against Rebecca Smith.

# 12

'Just vengeance does not call
for punishment.'

Corneille, *Le Cid* (1636)

# A CAD AND A
# BOUNDER

Judge's wife Valerie Harkess and her two attractive married daughters were filled with dread the day they discovered that one-time British MP and Tory minister Alan Clark was planning to publish his memoirs. For all three had, at one time, been seduced by the millionaire politician and they feared that their reputations would be irreparably damaged if he revealed any details about the sex romps all of them had experienced with Clark, a self-confessed lothario.

As the publication date of Clark's tell-all diaries rapidly approached, Valerie consoled and comforted her younger daughter Josephine, aged thirty-four, who was particularly distraught at the prospect of having her name publicised. Valerie's other daughter Alison had married and settled down in a different corner of the world and wanted nothing to do with the entire scenario.

Valerie and Josephine feared Old Etonian Clark was going to make references to his sexual liaisons with all three, describing them proudly as sex games ... and not obliquely enough to conceal the Harkess family name.

Valerie even contacted Clark and asked him if the auto-biography made any mention of her and her daughters. The one-time minister assured her that they were not mentioned by name.

When Valerie picked up a copy of the book as soon as it was published in her new home in South Africa, she was outraged. He had jokingly referred to a mother and daughter as his 'coven'. Valerie and her daughter felt betrayed. Valerie might be now enjoying a very privileged lifestyle in a forti-fied, white, gabled house called Raphael in Constantia, one of Cape Town's most prosperous suburbs, but that did not make it any easier to handle.

It was then that Valerie and Josephine decided to initiate one of the most extraordinary examples of female revenge ever witnessed in Britain. Rather than face an embarrassing whispering campaign, they revealed the full sordid details of their bedtime exploits with Clark to Britain's raciest, most-read tabloid newspaper, the *News of the World*.

In a remarkable cloak-and-dagger operation, *News of the World* journalists flew secretly to the Harkess home in South Africa where they were told an extraordinary account of sexual promiscuity at the very top of the Tory party. Valerie Harkess told the paper: 'Alan has virtually ruined all our lives, mine, my husband's and my two daughters'. He is a depraved animal.'

So it was with these words that Valerie and Josephine Harkess launched their bitter battle to expose casanova Alan Clark as one of the most notorious womanisers seen in British politics this century. They claimed they had endured years of sordid sex with the kinky former MP. Among the tamer claims against millionaire Clark was that he used Valerie for afternoon sex sessions in his flat near the House of Commons, and that he seduced Josephine's sister Alison when she was going through a particularly difficult time in her life.

Clark was also accused of taking advantage of Valerie's other daughter Josephine after she had been to see Clark to ask for his help. Other assorted claims were also made against Clark by the women. It all added up to a very sordid package for the *News of the World*.

Married Clark allegedly worked his way through the Harkess family during a fourteen-year affair with Valerie. By deciding to reveal the truth about the smutty one-time cabinet member, Valerie found herself having to confess her adultery to her husband James.

For some reason, her husband decided not to leave his cheating wife. She explained in breathless tones: 'I'd feared James might take it badly and leave us, but he's a wonderful, tolerant and forgiving Christian man. Our marriage is intact. I know it will take years for us to build the trust up again but we intend to do it.

'I expect no sympathy for my actions, nor for those of my daughters, but had it not been for these foul diaries, I might have taken the secret of my affair with Alan to my grave.'

Valerie and her daughter continued on the warpath against Clark by flying into London from South Africa to disclose more of the former politician's most sensitive secrets. Those included a series of letters and cards which gave an astonishing insight into the mind of the man who became one of Margaret Thatcher's most trusted confidants.

The Harkess family had already employed the services of one Max Clifford, a renowned publicist without whom no tawdry political scandal was complete in the 1990s. Just hours before the family flew into London's Heathrow Airport, Clifford proudly announced: 'The circus is coming into town.' Valerie and her clan were not going to let the matter just fizzle out. She and her husband talked about confronting Clark.

The *News of the World*'s decision to splash the women's extraordinary story across many pages of their edition on Sunday, 29 May 1994, was just the tip of the iceberg. Within days, the Harkess women were accused of being 'below-stairs types' by Clark's proud wife Jane, responding to reporters' questions outside the family's vast castle in Kent. However, Valerie and Josephine came back with a vengeance.

Valerie, at fifty-six still a very attractive woman, decided to exact every last drop of revenge by telling an even more detailed account of her fourteen-year affair with Clark to *The Sun* newspaper on 1 June 1994. She disclosed how she first met Clark when she was an eighteen-year-old law student and how he made a pass at her when he dined with her and her then husband at London's upmarket Grosvenor House

Hotel. Valerie even told how Clark ingratiated himself into her family to such a degree that her own husband encouraged her to go out for lunch with the Tory MP.

Eventually, she gave in to his demands and made love with Clark in his brother's house in London. Twisting the knife of revenge as sharply as she could, Valerie revealed: 'He was a very straight lover, but he was very selfish. He was only interested in his own satisfaction and he didn't bother with foreplay.'

The affair continued for another ten years, on and off, until Valerie visited London from her family's new home in South Africa and discovered that her elder daughter Alison was sleeping with Clark.

'I felt physically sick, and full of blame for my daughter being seduced,' she informed the world.

Yet, despite her disgust at discovering that her daughter was sleeping with her illicit lover, Valerie continued having sex sessions with Clark.

In 1983 – with Clark now firmly entrenched as a junior minister and one of Margaret Thatcher's most trusted advisers – he invited his secret married lover out for dinner with her other daughter Josephine. Then, in front of Clark, Josephine broke down and confessed that she, too, had been having an affair with Clark.

'The pain was so bad that if Jo hadn't been there I might have killed him with my bare hands,' insisted Valerie years later.

Despite her outrage, Valerie admitted that she continued to be addicted to Clark – and a year later she went to bed with him again.

'He dismissed what had happened as if it had just been a natural progression. I felt I was an adulterous wife, a bad mother and a worthless person. I was almost beyond caring what I thought of myself any more and blindly I slept with him a few more times almost like a zombie.'

Finally, in the late eighties, Valerie started to see the light as far as Alan Clark was concerned. In wonderfully explicit terms she explained: 'I realised for the first time what rotten teeth he had. They were like nasty pebbles and his face showed a shifty, ageing man kidding himself he was attractive to women.

'This shrivelled husk then had the nerve to suggest we went to bed once more. I said no, and walked out of his life.'

With a final swipe at her one-time bed partner, Valerie added: 'I hate Alan Clark for ever being born.'

Next it was Josephine's turn to exact her revenge upon the bed-hopping Tory. She claimed Clark had seduced her when was in a drunken stupor and insisted he took advantage of her when she turned to him for support as she battled alcohol addiction.

'I turned to Alan for comfort – he was Mother's friend, he had known me since I was a child. What I got were a few minutes of sex, sex I cannot even remember because of the condition I was in. I can remember feeling dirty. He made me feel like a dog.'

Despite her earlier 'disgust', the following night Josephine slept with Clark again. However, Clark was a bitter disappointment, which was much the same emotion her mother had felt after her first few sexual encounters with him.

Sticking the knife firmly into Clark, Josephine uttered the damning words: 'He seduced me when I was at my most vulnerable and when he knew I had no defences. That is something I cannot forgive him for. Alan obviously thought that because of his power, money and position he could expose us to ridicule and get away with it. Well he bloody well can't.'

Even Valerie's long-suffering husband, former Judge James Harkess, got in on the act by insisting: 'Valerie and I are more than just husband and wife. We are best friends, too, and nothing can destroy that. Certainly not a sick and sexually depraved man like Alan Clark.'

Just to make his point absolutely clearly to the world, Mr Harkess posed for *The Sun* newspaper with a horsewhip in one hand and a promise to use it on Alan Clark if he had the opportunity.

Alan Clark even managed to embroil his own long-suffering wife Jane in the scandal when she swiftly launched a loyal counter-attack. Breaking off from feeding the chickens at the couple's Saltwood Castle home, she told reporters that hints from the Harkess women that Clark had offered to buy their silence were absolutely not true.

'I was so cross when I heard that's what they were saying that I had to come straight down here and tell you the truth.' Mrs Clark said that, despite her husband's numerous confessions of infidelity, she still stood by him. It was an astonishing statement when one considers that she married him when she was just sixteen (he was thirty) and had somehow survived almost forty years of his philandering. She even told one friend a few days later that she considered his other women as 'bluebottles' whom she would like to crush.

Clark himself rounded off the entire circus by admitting he deserved a horsewhipping. 'It's a bit old-fashioned, but I suppose what I did deserves it.'

# 13

'Revenge proves its own executioner.'

John Ford, *The Broken Heart* (1633)

# THE TEXAS
# SHE-DEVIL

Lindale, in Texas, is one of those places where nothing ever seems to happen, despite the roar of Highway 69 through its heart. There are few men about on weekday mornings, apart from the occasional old boy in one of the sleazy bars on the edge of town or a gaggle of hearty young networkers playing golf on the local course. Most husbands head off to the nearby big cities for work. For the women there are open days at the school, knitting classes, and lots of good deeds to be done.

Jennifer Loving's life appeared normal enough. Her hard-working husband left for work early and got back after dark most nights. They were comfortable financially, but she did find she frequently had a little too much spare time.

Television programmes like *Married With Children* were watched avidly by Jennifer Loving, especially on those long, lonely evenings when her husband Greg decided to down endless beers in one of the local hostelries. Jennifer read little – magazines like the *National Enquirer* were her staple diet. Her chief occupation was bringing up their four-year-old son and going into town to do the shopping. She often spun those trips out most of the day. But there was another aspect to Jennifer's life that she never revealed to anyone; her husband's appalling temper tantrums. Well, that was what they were to start with, but soon they developed into something far worse . . .

'Get a fucking move on, woman!'

Greg Loving was waiting outside the bathroom as his wife sat on the toilet. At times, it seemed as if there was no escape, no sanctuary from him.

'I said. Get outta there.'

Suddenly the door burst open and Greg snatched the ragged remains of the toilet roll on the sink next to Jennifer.

'I told you not to use so much goddamn paper, woman!'

Jennifer looked up at him in terror. She had seen that look in his eyes before. They were deep and dark and distant and she knew that meant he was about to beat her. She was trembling. He jerked her off the toilet, bent her over his knee and spanked her naked bottom so hard she could feel the stinging all the way down to her ankles.

'I told you not to use so much goddamn paper woman. I told you!'

He beat her for ten minutes. His breathing became irregular. She sensed he wasn't just using his anger to punish her. She suspected he was getting his kicks from humiliating her. She did not dare struggle because then he would hit her even harder. Finally, he pushed her from his lap and shoved her to the floor. Her bottom was covered in bruises. She began to wonder where it would all end.

It wasn't the first time she had been beaten by Greg and she was certain it would not be the last. Sometimes he would smash her around the living room with his fists, then force her into the bedroom where he would rape her all night long.

When Jennifer told some of her friends in town they said he could not have raped her because he was her husband. Jennifer assured them he did. But the women of Lindale did not really want to know.

This quiet, sleepy town with its population of just 2,500, was renowned as a place where nothing much happened and that was the way everyone in Lindale wanted to keep it. Even when the beatings and sexual attacks grew worse, Jennifer accepted them as part of married life. In any case there were other occasions when Gary could be so pleasant and loving. Sometimes, he would take Jennifer and their son out for picnics in the country. On other occasions, he would shower them with gifts. It was often hard for Jennifer to work out where the good Gary ended and the bad Gary began. She had thought it was connected to alcohol at first, but he eventually began to attack her even when he was stone cold sober.

Other times, Gary himself would recognise he was about to go crazy and he would charge into the back yard or jump in his pick-up to get away, so he could cool off without taking it out on his frail young wife. But one day, in early August 1992, Gary came home from work in a filthy mood. He was ranting and raving about everything from the cost of the shopping to Jennifer's excessive use of washing powder. She tried to walk away from him, but he grabbed her wrist and pulled her down onto his lap. She presumed another beating was about to happen.

But Gary's lip curled up as he looked into her eyes. She tried to look away but she could feel his glare boring into her. Those eyes were nasty, deep and emotionless. They were scaring her. He sat there holding her down on his lap like that for at least five minutes, just silently trying to out-stare his petrified wife. Every time she tried to look away he squeezed her wrist tightly then pulled her round again.

Suddenly he pulled a gun out of his pocket and shoved it to her temple.

*This is it*, thought Jennifer. *He is going to kill me. It's been on the cards for long enough. Now the time has come. 'Oh, God make it quick. Please make it quick.'*

Jennifer closed her eyes and waited for it to happen. But only silence followed. Then she felt the cold metal of the gun's snub pushing at her mouth.

'Open up, bitch.'

Jennifer was so scared she did nothing at first.

'Open up, BITCH!'

She parted her mouth and felt the cold steel slide between her lips. After pushing three inches of the barrel in, he began easing it backwards and forwards. In and out. She kept her eyes closed throughout. Jennifer could hear her husband's breathing quickening. She dared not think about the perverted images that must have been going through his mind at that moment.

'You want it, don't you, bitch?'

Then, just as suddenly, he shoved much more of the barrel into her mouth and stopped. It was choking her. She presumed he was about to pull the trigger.

CLICK. He pulled.

*This is it*, she thought. But nothing happened. He was laughing.

'Say bye-bye.'

CLICK. He pulled the trigger.

Nothing happened. He was laughing uncontrollably now. With a quick jerk, he pulled the barrel out from between her lips, scraping her teeth in the process.

'Open your eyes. You're still alive.'

A few days later, Jennifer discovered that she was pregnant. To most married couples this would have been great news, but to Jennifer it represented danger because she was going to have to tell Greg and there was no knowing exactly how he would respond. Just before he came home she managed to find the same gun with which Greg had simulated death and oral sex on her, and made sure it was loaded. This time he was not going to hurt her.

'Shit. That's bad news,' were the first words Greg spoke after Jennifer told him the news of her pregnancy as they sat in the back yard.

'Whose is it, anyhow?'

Jennifer was too frightened to answer.

'I think I'll take the kid and get outta here, now! You whore.'

The words wounded Jennifer. There was no way she would allow him to take their son, and how dare he suggest she was having sex with anyone other than him. He had made these sorts of threats before, but this time he wasn't going to get away with it.

Then she saw that look in his eyes once more and knew trouble was on the horizon. She could feel her hands shaking. She didn't know what to do. Then Greg Loving signed his own death sentence. He began running towards her. She hesitated, but saw those eyes snapping at her and instantly knew she had to do it. Jennifer raised the semi-automatic pistol, aimed right at her husband and squeezed the trigger. This time the gun was loaded. The bullet pierced his head and he crumpled to the ground.

Minutes later, Jennifer somehow managed to hoist her bleeding husband on to the flatbed of his precious pick-up truck. Every now and again he mumbled a few words incoherently.

*That's a relief,* thought Jennifer. *I want him to stay alive a bit longer. I want him to really suffer.*

Jennifer rushed into the house, grabbed her four-year-old son and placed him in the front seat next to her. She decided to drive 50 miles to her relatives in the city of Longview. That would mean her husband had a slow and painful death as she drove along the bumpy highway. In fact, every time she hit a pothole she smiled to herself because she knew that would increase his pain.

. . .

Police officer Sherryl Bolton chose to make law enforcement

his career in 1989. He settled in Lindale because he wanted to avoid the big city death and destruction that exists in most of the United States. This was going to be the perfect place to work and raise a family. A private, shy man, Bolton had no desire for glory just a genuine interest in the good of the common man. He had left his native state of Louisiana and lived for a while in Houston, Texas, a metropolitan area besieged by crime. In Houston, Bolton was shocked by the blatant disregard for the law. It seemed as if no-one cared. The daily onslaught of death and destruction convinced Bolton that he was in need of somewhere more gentle and he figured a small town like Lindale would be the perfect place for him to contribute to keeping the peace.

Lindale's Chief of Police, Mike Rutherford, was a veteran cop, who considered Bolton to be a fine officer. His quiet, cautious habits were well appreciated in the town where rip-roaring cowboy behaviour was definitely not appreciated. Rutherford knew that Sherryl Bolton was more than capable of handling a big case if required.

Life in Lindale seemed as peaceful as ever on the hot, sticky night of August 10, 1992. The trees in the pine woods surrounding the town were creaking in the scorching heat. In the distance there was an occasional rumble from one of the big 18-wheel tractor-trailer rigs negotiating the red lights as they rushed through town on Highway 69. Frequently, the backfires and blowouts from the 18-wheelers could sound like gunshots. So, when a loud pop rang through the air at 9:30pm that night, no one gave it a second thought.

Fifty miles away, in the metropolis of Longview, Texas

(pop 50,000), law officers were dealing with the sort of crimes that Sherryl Bolton hated. Dispatchers and cops were breaking up domestic incidents, shutting down rowdy bars, plucking accident victims off the streets and dealing with a string of burglaries. When the Longview Police Department was called out to a shooting on the edge of the city, it was nothing unusual. There were about a dozen such incidents every month in the city. Dead at the scene was Greg Loving, a 39-year-old self employed construction worker, the son of the former postmaster of the smaller town of Lindale. Loving's brother-in-law had called police to tell them about a body which had showed up at his residence. He had not even realised at first glance that it was a relative.

Longview investigators found Loving's corpse sprawled in the back of his pick-up truck parked out front of the house. Pools of blood filled the bed of the truck. Also at the scene was Greg Loving's wife Jennifer. She calmly explained to police that her husband had been despondent and had shot himself, following a family argument. She told the officers all this in a manner that suggested complete control of the situation. There were no tears, there was little emotion, just a very matter-of-fact style delivery. It was almost as if she was talking about someone who was not even related to her. In fact, she was describing the scene as if she was a cop.

Longview police Lieutenant Mike Satterwhite was puzzled by the apparent coolness of the victim's wife. It bothered him a great deal, but for the moment he had nothing more than a hunch to go on. In his mind he couldn't say for certain whether it was murder or suicide. He was also deeply bothered by the fact that it appeared that Greg

Loving had been shot several hours earlier. Why hadn't the police been called sooner? And why didn't they take Loving to the hospital? After taking a statement from 25-year-old Jennifer Loving, police in Lindale were notified of the killing because that was where the Lovings lived. Lt. Satterwhite advised Lindale that they should handle the investigation because he firmly believed the shooting had taken place at the Lovings' home the previous evening. In Lindale, Chief Rutherford was puzzled by the request to take over the investigation, but decided that he should put Sherryl Bolton on the case anyhow. For Bolton – awakened in the middle of the night and told he was chief investigator on a homicide inquiry – it was a baptism of fire. He had never been involved in a murder investigation and, to make matters worse, this one had actually ended in a city fifty miles away.

But within hours, Bolton and crime scene investigator Jason Waller were reviewing all the information they had on the case. They rapidly concluded that they should ask for a warrant to search the Lovings' neat, detached house in the older section on the east side of town. Jennifer Loving did not bat an eyelid when Bolton and his team knocked on her front door and demanded entry to the house. The officers combed the area very carefully and soon uncovered several weapons, including a .22 calibre semi-automatic pistol hidden under a mattress in the couple's bedroom. They immediately brought Mrs Loving in for questioning.

At first, the grieving wife retold the same suicide story she had given the Longview police the previous night.

'We were drinking beer about 10 o'clock in the evening

and I told Greg I was pregnant again,' she explained quietly and calmly. 'He got angry and went into the back yard to be alone.'

Greg, she explained to the officers, always liked to be alone when he was upset. Jennifer insisted that Greg had been completely thrown by the news of impending fatherhood because he wasn't ready to have another child 'just now'. Jennifer then lowered her voice to a virtual whisper as she told officers that she stayed inside the house for half an hour more with their four-year-old son while Greg continued sulking outside. Later, she became curious when Greg did not come back inside the house. She claimed that, when she finally decided to look for him, she found him slumped unconscious over the tailgate of their pick-up truck. Greg had shot himself. She said she had heard a pop earlier, but ignored it because she thought it was a firecracker or one of those trucks thundering through town.

'I found him in the back of the pick-up and he looked like he was dead. I checked him for a pulse and I could not find one. I figured he had shot himself in the head because he had blood on his face and I found a gun laying on the ground.'

Then Jennifer switched the subject around to herself. It startled the investigators. 'I didn't shoot my husband and I don't think anyone else did.'

Officer Bolton was intrigued by this response because it certainly seemed to suggest that Jennifer had a guilty conscience, if nothing else. She then told in vivid detail how she pushed his body onto the rough metal flatbed of the truck and began to drive towards Longview, where her closest relatives lived. She believed that her brother would know what to do and would calm her down. She did not have any place else to turn.

But, as the questioning continued, more and more inconsistencies emerged in her story. Investigators were soon in absolutely no doubt that she was covering up the truth. Jennifer became more and more nervous. Suddenly, she cracked and broke down and cried. She admitted pulling the trigger of the gun but insisted it had gone off unexpectedly in her hands. The young wife then said she had become upset when she thought Greg was going to move away and take their son with him. She admitted being a little drunk, but continued to insist the shooting was an accident.

But, when investigators questioned other family and friends, they dismissed her claims yet again especially since police had been called to the residence to break up numerous domestic disputes. Jennifer also had her fair share of drinking trophies. These included a conviction for Driving While Intoxicated in neighbouring Wood County. She was still serving felony probation for that offence at the time of her husband's shooting.

Eventually, the investigators uncovered enough evidence to bring the case before a Grand Jury. Officer Bolton and Sgt. David Craft of the Lindale Police Department obtained a warrant for her arrest. A bond was set at $40,000.

In November 1993, the murder trial of Jennifer Loving was held in the 7th District Court of Judge Louis Gohmert, a young attorney who had just been elected to the bench. The trial was heard in the Smith County Courthouse in Tyler, about 15 miles north of Lindale. By the time proceedings had begun Jennifer had changed her story again. She now admitted the shooting had not been an accident, but she pleaded self-defence to the murder charge, on the basis that her husband had been violent to her when she told him she thought she might be pregnant.

One of the prime defence witnesses was Dr Robert Geffner of the Family Violence and Sexual Assault Institute. Dr Geffner testified that he believed Jennifer had Battered Woman's Syndrome and that her mental problems and severe stress had been caused by the abuse that led to the shooting. The doctor described the condition as causing a 'numbing where they (the women) psychologically numb themselves not to feel'. Dr Geffner added, 'When the syndrome strikes the woman blacks out her thoughts in a psychological amnesia where it's so painful the brain tries to keep certain thoughts out of the mind.'

Dr Geffner, who is also a psychology professor at the University of Texas at Tyler, said Jennifer appeared to have been physically, mentally and sexually abused. His official diagnosis had been developed over a nine-month period and included some 15 separate tests. He also indicated she was suffering from "post traumatic stress disorder" as a result of the shooting. The doctor insisted that Jennifer was in a confused mental state that night and 'it took her a long time to realize what shape the victim was in.'

In her statement to Lindale Police, Jennifer had said, 'I kept expecting him to get up and beat me.' The defence team noted that the post traumatic stress disorder would explain her peculiar actions that night when she left Greg in the truck. Jennifer's defence attorney also gave the court examples of appalling episodes described to him by Jennifer. Several of the incidents involved her claims of forced sex and beatings.

The physician noted that, despite what happened, 'to this day it appears she still loves him and wishes the shooting hadn't happened. She wanted them to remain as a family. She just didn't want to be hit any more.' Prosecutors insisted that Jennifer Loving was more than capable of looking after herself and they brought in several witnesses who testified to her own violent behaviour. One neighbour had the court in laughter when she said, 'If Jennifer went into the woods hunting bear with a toothpick, she'd come out the winner.'

Prosecutors argued that Jennifer carefully set up the murder and intended to carry Greg's body to Longview to dispose of it, until relatives intervened and called in the police. They also insisted that Jennifer should have sought a divorce from her husband if she had been as badly beaten as she claimed.

The jury deliberated for five hours, before returning a guilty verdict. The ten women and two men on the jury did not believe that her response to her brutal husband had been justifiable. After another four hours of deliberation, jurors assessed Jennifer's punishment at 92 years in prison. They chose the number 92 to remind Jennifer of the year she murdered her husband.

*FOOTNOTE: This remarkable case took one more turn before it could be closed. Jennifer was placed in the Smith County Jail, in Tyler, to await her transfer to the state prison.*

*When she and several other female inmates returned from the exercise yard, Jennifer saw an opportunity to escape. She slipped her small wrists out of her handcuffs and broke into a run. The startled guard escorting the inmates decided to stay with the other prisoners rather than give chase. Loving rapidly discarded her orange jail uniform and bolted through the front door of the courthouse, which is equipped with bars and locked only from the outside, in compliance with fire regulations. Police were soon in hot pursuit as the other inmates cheered Jennifer on, who soon became lost in the crowds on the streets of downtown Tyler.*

*The Sheriff's department in Lindale was immediately notified of the escape and police surveillance was put on the Lovings' house. Officer Bolton was deeply disappointed that Jennifer had escaped. But Jennifer Loving wanted no part of Lindale after all the beatings and abuse she had suffered at the hands of her husband in that small town. She headed in the opposite direction. Jennifer had sneaked to a downtown Tyler church, wearing only white boxer shorts and a T-shirt. There she had made several phone calls and found extra clothing. Then she and a boyfriend headed to a motel 15 miles outside Tyler. Acting on an anonymous tip, officers tracked down Loving and arrested her – it was just five hours after her escape.*

*Jennifer's only comment when caught was, 'Okay, you got me.' She smiled broadly at photographers and news reporters as officers placed her in handcuffs and led her back to jail. District Attorney Skeen filed charges of felony escape, a third-degree felony punishable by two to ten years in prison and a fine of up to $5,000 upon conviction. Meanwhile, Sherryl Bolton earned his own reward for bringing Jennifer to justice. The* *young officer was chosen by the Lindale City Council to be the new Chief of Police in the town.*

In the eyes of many women, Jennifer Loving is not a criminal, but a heroine who took the law into her own hands . . .

# 14

'*Revenge is a luscious fruit which you must leave to ripen.*'

Emile Gaboriau, *File 113 (1867)*

# A LOVE THAT
# WOULD NOT DIE

Ivor Stokle and Pauline Leyshon met when they were both working at a factory making fuel-injection systems. At the time, he was still sharing a home with Sheila Stroud, his girlfriend of ten years, but that relationship was effectively over as they were sleeping in separate bedrooms and Sheila had even moved an old boyfriend back into the house.

As far as Ivor was concerned, the only thing he still had in common with Sheila was the ownership of their property in Rudford, Gloucestershire, which they had bought jointly some years earlier. He knew that the end of their association would finally come when she agreed to a fair payout of his share of the value of the house. Then they could go their separate ways.

However, things were much more complicated for Ivor's new lover, Pauline, aged forty-two. She was still living with her husband Ken. They had four grown-up children and all the complications that go with such a large family. Through more than twenty years of marriage, she had never imagined she would ever fall in love with another man but, in the end, she concluded that she and Ken were not going anywhere in life together, and she was growing increasingly unhappy – until thirty-two-year-old Ivor came along.

At first they carried on their clandestine affair at the factory in great secrecy, making sure that no one was hurt by the relationship. By May 1991, however, their love for each other was proving so strong that both agreed it was time to move in together, so they rented a small flat in Gloucester, where they were very happy.

For the following few months life seemed to get better and better for the couple. Eventually, they found a bungalow that would make the perfect buy to seal their relationship. Ivor went to see Sheila to try to iron out a deal to get her to buy him out of the property they owned.

However, Sheila had money problems and immediately began to drag her feet about giving Ivor the £20,000 he knew was his share of that house. She told him that her business was in difficulties and that she and her current lover, Mark Evans, were in no position to give Ivor the money.

The couple had bought the property for £141,500 with a mortgage of £99,000. They had jointly taken out two life-insurance policies and an endowment policy, which meant that if one died the other would receive £108,900. Ivor had even made sure that Sheila knew that, on his death, his employers' insurance policy was worth a further £30,000.

To begin with, Ivor was very understanding about his ex-lover's dilemma and told Sheila that she could have a while longer to sort out the money situation. None the less, Ivor had a nagging feeling in the back of his mind; he was starting not to trust Sheila's word. After all, she had betrayed him in the ultimate fashion by moving Mark in as a lodger and then having an illicit relationship with him under his nose.

Ivor had never forgotten how he once came home early from his job at the factory to find Sheila and Mark making love in the bed he was supposed to be sharing with her. It was shortly after that when Ivor moved his belongings into the spare room to endure months of living under the same roof with his long-time lover and her new bedmate. It was a humiliating experience for Ivor, especially at night when he could hear their love making through the thin walls ...

By November 1991, Ivor had decided he could not wait any longer to settle the financial situation with Sheila. Pauline had rightly pointed out that he did not exactly owe Sheila any favours. After all, she was the one who had betrayed him so hurtfully.

Ivor arranged for Sheila and him to see a solicitor to sort out the money. Then on 14 November – the day before they were due to see the lawyer – Sheila phoned Ivor and asked him if he and Pauline would meet her in a pub early next day. Perhaps naively, Ivor presumed that his former lover was actually intending to sort out the house money. When Ivor and Pauline got to the pub, however, Sheila insisted that they go back to the house to meet Mark. The couple drove back behind her.

At the house, Sheila seemed calm and very charming, even giving her one-time lover and his new girlfriend a cup of tea. Ivor did not even think it strange when Mark tried to persuade him to go out to the garage to pick up a battery charger he had left behind when he moved out.

'Just leave it by my car. I'll pick it up when we go,' Ivor told the man who had earlier stolen his lover from him.

Just then, Sheila and Mark got up and left the sitting room. Ivor looked at Pauline with a puzzled expression on his face. Where were they going? She shrugged her shoulders.

Suddenly, a black-hooded man burst through the door brandishing a knife. Pauline managed to scramble for the door and headed towards the hallway. Meanwhile, the man – Norman White – forced Ivor to the floor at knife point. Ivor felt the cold blade of the weapon pressing into the back of his neck. As White put his foot on the back of Ivor's neck, Ivor looked up and he got the shock of his life – Sheila and Mark Evans were helping to tie him up.

'This'll teach you to shit on me,' she muttered before Ivor's jumper was pulled up over his head.

Seconds later, Pauline was forced to the floor next to Ivor and kicked viciously in the side and the face. She was screaming hysterically.

The couple were then frog-marched outside and loaded into the pick-up truck that Sheila used for her business. Ivor tried desperately to calm Pauline down but she could not stop sobbing. He also struggled with the ropes holding his hands behind his back, managing partially to loosen them.

Ivor was terrified. He presumed that his ex-lover, her boyfriend and this other man were planning to dump Pauline and him in some isolated spot in the country. Then it dawned on him that they must be intending a much worse fate.

For what seemed like hours, the hog-tied, blindfolded couple were driven around. Ivor could clearly hear the engine of his own car, a Vauxhall Viva, behind them as they travelled. Then it seemed to fade into the distance.

Finally, the pick-up stopped and Ivor and Pauline were dragged out. Ivor could now see clearly and he immediately realised that they were at a well-known beauty spot, called Barrow Wake, which overlooked the city of Gloucester.

Suddenly, he was hit over the head with a jack. Crumpling to the ground, Ivor somehow managed to work out that it would be a good idea to pretend to be unconscious. He feared that another forceful blow might kill him, so he kept his eyes tightly closed, moaned and then acted dead.

Next to him, Pauline was hit viciously with a fence stake. Ivor heard it all but was powerless to do anything. He heard Pauline saying: 'Why are you doing this to us, Mark? We don't deserve this.'

Ivor's hands and feet were then retied securely with the ropes and he was bundled into the passenger seat of his own car. Next to him, Pauline was manhandled into the driver's seat. Learner-driver plates were attached to the car so that it would look as if the inexperienced driver, Pauline, had lost control of the vehicle.

Ivor knew full well that they were only feet from the

edge of the cliff. He heard the car being rammed with an almighty thud from behind. Suddenly, it started to roll forward.

'Flame ho!' shouted Mark Evans.

Just then a whooshing noise followed and Pauline screamed that the car was on fire. Within two or three seconds more, the vehicle was engulfed in flames. It was going over the verge and down towards the final drop.

Somehow, over the next few moments, Ivor swivelled his back against the passenger door and kicked hard three times with his feet, forcing Pauline's door open. Luckily, the driver's seat had been pulled out full to accommodate Ivor's long legs and Pauline, much shorter, was far enough back to allow a space for him to kick out at the door next to her. Finally, it burst open and they tumbled out on to the grass, their clothes and flesh smoking.

Seconds later, the Vauxhall Viva crashed 250 feet over the cliff. Ivor had absolutely no idea if Pauline was still in the vehicle. By that time – with his body in shock – he could feel no pain whatsoever. He could just make out car lights heading towards him and he staggered to a wall, hiding behind it in case it was his assailants returning to finish off the job.

However, it turned out that a motorist had spotted the bright orange glow and had rung the emergency services. At first, he had thought it was some kind of UFO.

The lights that Ivor saw belonged to a police car. Ivor struggled towards it, the ropes that bound him hanging at his side. 'Don't lose the ropes. Don't lose the ropes. They're evidence.' Somehow, through the excruciating pain,

Ivor managed to make himself remember those words.

'Help me. Help me,' he muttered at the approaching emergency-service personnel. 'My girlfriend has been murdered. She is in the car.'

Ivor slumped into the rear passenger door of a police car. Smoke was coming off his clothing. The rope was still tied under his arms, around his torso and around his neck.

Just then PC David Spencer heard someone moaning in what he later described as in a way that was like something out of a horror film. The policeman aimed his torch in that direction and saw a human shape coming towards him. The figure's clothes were partly burned off and the left side of the face and the hair were blackened. As the figure collapsed into his arms he finally realised he was dealing with a woman.

Seconds later, fireman Dave Baldwin plunged Ivor's hands into buckets of cold water and ordered more water to be poured over his head. It was prompt action which probably saved Ivor's hands and face but all Ivor cared about was Pauline. In tears, he told the police that she must have gone over the edge of the cliff in the car. Unknown to him, Pauline was already in safe hands.

The couple were immediately rushed to the burns unit at Frenchay Hospital in Bristol. Ivor's family were warned that he might not survive the weekend. He was unconscious for six days.

Meanwhile, Pauline – who had forty per cent burns – was so badly disfigured that when her own daughter first saw her she didn't recognise her. However, the couple had tremendous will to survive. Their love for one another was so strong that they did not want to be parted.

Looking back on that appalling night, Ivor is still astonished by how rapidly he reacted. 'In a crisis you find resources you don't know you've got.'

In Frenchay Hospital, both faced a long battle to recover from their injuries. Pauline had been wearing thinner clothes so she had more burns, but some of Ivor's went deeper. At one stage it looked as if Pauline's left arm would have to be amputated.

She lost thirty per cent of her scalp and had six operations to get her hair to grow across the new skin. She later had another two operations in 1994. Immediately after the incident, Pauline suffered from severe depression and became suicidal. She lost two stone in two weeks while in hospital and the staff there feared she had lost the will to live. She later admitted that she was terrified of seeing the state of her injuries.

Ivor's face was badly burned. His right arm was burned to above the elbow, as were his shins and knees and parts of his body. He also lost fifty per cent of the hearing in his right ear.

Incredibly, though, his injuries actually improved his eyesight and he no longer wears the glasses he used for his shortsightedness. Stranger still, he has started to grow again and is now an inch and a quarter taller than before. However, his lungs have been permanently damaged from inhaling smoke and fumes. On his badly burned right arm, he still has the marks from the ropes used to tie him.

It was two months before the two were allowed home from hospital, with only one pair of hands between them – 'Ivor's left and my right,' says Pauline.

More than a year after the horrific attack, Ivor and

Pauline attended the trial of Sheila Stroud, aged thirty-three, Mark Evans, thirty-two, and Norman White, thirty-one, at Bristol Crown Court where they faced charges of kidnapping and attempted murder.

Stroud and Evans were said to have recruited unemployed Norman White into their plot. Prosecutor Alun Jenkins said White claimed Stroud 'offered to pay him £30,000 to kill her ex-boyfriend'. White was asked by his own girlfriend Rae Crowhurst if he was going to do it.

Mr Jenkins explained: 'He said he wouldn't; he would seriously hurt him. But you don't get payouts on life assurance policies for seriously hurting someone.'

The judge at the trial described the actions of all three as 'in the higher echelons of wickedness and crime'.

It was revealed that, two weeks before the incident, Stroud and Evans watched a television film entitled *Fighting Mad*. The jury was shown a clip from the movie in which a young couple were kidnapped, tied up and placed in their car, which was pushed over a quarry edge and set alight, killing them.

'I looked at them and felt absolutely nothing,' Ivor recalled. 'It is very strange to know that you lived with someone for ten years only to find they plotted to kill you.' All three were sentenced to eighteen years in prison.

.    .    .

Pauline and Ivor finally bought their dream bungalow in the picturesque Gloucestershire village of Frampton-on-Severn. Explained Pauline, 'Our attitude to life has changed. We appreciate every day. When bills arrive, we don't panic.' The couple have each received £25,000 from the Criminal Injuries Compensation Board and there will be further money to follow.

On 24 September 1994, Pauline and Ivor were thrilled when their consultant, Andrew Burd, agreed to give Pauline away at their dream wedding. A crowd of staff from Frenchay Hospital turned up as guests, along with fireman Dave Baldwin. Pauline's two daughters, twenty-five-year-old Sonia and twenty-three-year-old Claire were bridesmaids, as were her three granddaughters. Her one grandson was a pageboy. Her two sons, Craig, twenty-one, and Shen, twenty, were ushers.

# 15

*'It is difficult to fight against anger; for a man will buy revenge with his soul'.*

*Heraclitus (500 BC)*

# A FONDNESS
# FOR
# YOUNG LADIES

Former magistrate Graham Partridge still had a keen eye for the ladies, even though he was pushing seventy-five years of age. Long since parted from his invalid wife, he simply thrived in the company of women, most of whom were at least forty years his junior. To Graham Partridge, the female members of the species were there to honour and obey him, especially when it came to the bedroom.

It was hardly surprising, therefore, when Graham's attention was caught by a familiar-looking woman waiting on the corner of the street near her home in the west Wales town of Llangoedmor. As his eyes panned up and down her rather shapely body, he realised that she was an attractive redhead whom he used to see going into her ballet school opposite his office years previously. Graham Partridge never forgot a pretty face. This was too good an opportunity for Graham to pass up. He stopped his car, rolled down the window and offered the woman a lift.

Kathryn George-Harries was flattered by the old man's attention and readily accepted. She later realised that when she got into his car that morning, she somehow instantly knew that they were about to embark on a relationship.

Kathryn was already vaguely acquainted with Graham through her family's business dealings with the ex-JP. He was a highly respected member of the small, rural community in which they both lived. Twice Graham had even stood as Conservative parliamentary candidate for the area.

At twenty-five, and considering that she was in the middle of training to be a solicitor, Kathryn happened to be a very vulnerable, unworldly woman. Perhaps that was what attracted Graham Partridge to her. He could mould her into whatever he wanted her to be, whenever he wanted. She had a kind of sensitivity which he immediately decided to capitalise on.

Kathryn was entranced by Graham as they drove together that morning. She did not realise he was so old and thought he was in his early sixties. In any case, he had the looks of a younger man and a sparkle in his eye which tantalised her from the moment they met.

Within weeks, Graham and Kathryn were enjoying a tempestuous sexual relationship conducted in absolute secrecy. He had insisted that no one knew about their affair because of their families' links and she had accepted his condition because it seemed reasonable considering there was such a vast age gap between them.

Love making was remarkably energetic and adventurous considering his age. Graham even revealed later that, before making love, Kathryn liked to tantalise him by caressing the long barrels of his collection of guns. She also really enjoyed lifting her skirt up to reveal 'legs that went on for ever'. He also claimed that she was always the one who begged him to have sex with her. Graham assured one friend that Kathryn was definitely GIB – good in bed.

However, after a few months of their twice-weekly romps at Graham's £500,000 farmhouse in nearby Carmarthen, Kathryn began to feel the strain of their constant ducking and diving to avoid the gossips of the village, many of whom were already well aware of Graham's fondness for young ladies.

She also felt constantly guilty about the relationship. She hated the fact that she was abusing her family's trust by hiding the truth from them. Kathryn had a secret life that she could not discuss with anyone and it was putting enormous strain on her.

Then there was all the juggling that had to be performed. They could never be seen out together in the area, so candle-lit, romantic meals in local restaurants were out of the question. Most times their 'romance' involved Kathryn sneaking into Graham's home and sharing a bottle of his vintage wine, followed by a rapid ascent to the master bedroom.

In many ways it was an insidious process. Gradually, it became as regular as clockwork and although Kathryn was well aware of the pointless nature of it all, she simply could not stop herself. Each time she tried to question the wisdom of conducting a clandestine affair with a man old enough to be her grandfather, she would find herself sucked back into his sexual web of complicity.

Kathryn knew she needed help and advice but she was up against an emotional brick wall. She couldn't discuss it with anyone because then she would be betraying his trust. As the months turned into a year, Kathryn realised that she had gone beyond breaking point and back again. It was like a huge vicious, never-ending sexual circle.

After about eighteen months, her affair with Graham became such a strain that she suffered regular bouts of exhaustion and was drained of all enthusiasm for anything other than those twice-weekly sex sessions at his house. Her judgement began to be impaired. She began to feel seething jealousy whenever she found any hint of other girlfriends at the house.

At first, she did not say anything to Graham but, as her suspicions grew, so did her complete and utter insecurity about their relationship. Although she knew full well that it could never end in marriage, she wanted to be his only woman. She wanted to prove to Graham Partridge that she was capable of being everything to him: lover, girlfriend, helper, friend.

However, Graham wasn't looking for anything other than an occasional bed partner and he preferred to have a few of those on tap at any one time to satisfy his sexual appetite and general lust for life. As he told one friend: 'I prefer the company of women after 6 p.m.' In other words, females were his staple diet. As long as he had the urge to make love, he wanted a whole harem in close proximity.

Sometimes Graham would drop hints to Kathryn which suggested she was over-awed by her older lover. Nothing could have been further from the truth. She was a well-qualified woman in the middle of studying for a professional career, not a square-bottomed peasant or one of the chiffon-clad darlings who she suspected were among the regular visitors to the Partridge bedroom when she was not around.

As Kathryn later explained: 'I come from a middle-class family and have never been impressed by wealth. In any case, he wasn't half as wealthy as people thought.'

Kathryn also later insisted that she never actually loved Graham Partridge although she was certainly growing completely obsessed with him. Part of that obsession was an ever-increasing expectancy that he should be faithful to her.

For his part, Graham was not particularly bothered. He sensed that she was getting too possessive and wanted to end the relationship nicely and calmly if she continued her obsessive behaviour. He believed that she was expecting too much from him. He feared she might want to move in with him and that was definitely not what Graham Partridge wanted. In his eyes, that was crossing the border of what any relationship meant to him. He actually believed that having sex twice a week with a woman almost fifty years his junior was nothing more than a 'laid-back friendship'. For all his experience with women, Graham did not really understand or appreciate them.

On the evening of 9 May 1990, Kathryn called at

Graham's farmhouse, expecting, naturally, to end up in his bedroom. Graham was not in so she decided to wait for him to return, presuming that they would, as usual, sleep together that night.

Then she heard a car coming up the driveway. As it approached she saw that Graham was being driven by another lady friend of his, called Patricia Plewes.

When he saw Kathryn waiting for him, Graham immediately sensed trouble. 'Oh my God, there goes my good night's sleep,' he thought. Typically charming, even in the face of such adversity, Graham invited both women into his house for a nightcap. That was his first mistake of the evening.

Within minutes of settling in the kitchen with a glass of wine each, Kathryn exploded. 'You're sleeping with him,' she accused Patricia Plewes.

Graham was appalled by what he heard and immediately insisted that Kathryn should leave the house. Then he considered the situation and realised that she would simply hang around outside until he let her in, so he asked Patricia to take him back to his friend's house where he had been earlier that night.

Kathryn was horrified. How could he be interested in such a ghastly woman? How could he betray their relationship so brazenly? How could he humiliate her in such a cruel manner?

Graham Partridge knew full well that Kathryn was about to 'blow her lid' at any moment. He got up. 'I'll be back in a while,' he told Kathryn before leaving the farmhouse with Patricia.

Kathryn never once questioned the honesty of the last words he uttered to her. She fully expected him to return to her so that they could retire to bed and reignite their passion for one another. She sat at the table of his vast kitchen and started counting the minutes. After half an hour, she decided to open a bottle of his best wine from the vast collection in the cellar.

Three hours later, Kathryn staggered to the phone on the kitchen wall and dialled the home of the woman who had driven off with Graham. When Patricia Plewes picked up the phone, Kathryn exploded with jealous rage and demanded that Graham Partridge come back immediately. 'Send Graham home. I'm tart number one,' Kathryn screamed at her rival before slamming the phone down.

By this time, Kathryn's mind was a scrambled mess of emotional turmoil. She kept thinking that what had happened with the other woman meant that she was nothing more than one of his many bits on the side. For the first time it was dawning on her that she meant very little to him. The hurt was overwhelming.

Kathryn now realised that material possessions were far more important to Graham Partridge than people. She looked around at all the valuable antiques in the house and decided that the best way to hurt him was to destroy his belongings. If she destroyed them, then she could destroy all the pain and hurt. Kathryn had been pushed around for too long. She was going to smash everything to pieces.

She started with the clothes in his wardrobes. That would punish the always dapper and immaculately turned-out Graham Partridge. Then her attention was drawn to the four-poster bed where she and Graham had made hot, passionate love so often. It had to be destroyed because it represented the very epicentre of their relationship. She jumped up and down on it more ferociously than during any of their love-making efforts. She pulled at the bedhead until it ripped away, then went back to jumping until the base snapped and the bed sagged. Then she staggered drunkenly back to the kitchen, took all the eggs from the fridge and smeared them over the walls.

Next she started systematically smashing every window in the house. Then she headed for the antiques in the drawing room. She was on a roller-coaster ride of drunken revenge and nothing was going to stop her. Brandishing a screwdriver and knife she slashed at the sofas and then waded into his finest china which stood sedately in a special display cupboard.

Kathryn just did not care any more. She had got to the point of no return.

After an hour and a half of non-stop destruction, in which she had injured herself quite seriously with all that flying glass and crockery, Kathryn stopped, satisfied that sufficient damage had been done to the man who had hurt her so badly. Only the cat and her china food bowl escaped Kathryn's violence.

When it was over she felt elated. She knew full well what the consequences of her actions would be but she didn't care. This was the best feeling in the world. He had got everything he deserved.

Kathryn was covered in blood and feathers but feeling absolutely wonderful, even liberated. She had exorcised everything that had happened to her during that two-year relationship.

She scrunched out of the house through piles of broken Doulton china and a sea of smashed glass with a look of sheer and complete satisfaction at a job well done. She had got to the end of her tether and dealt with her problem by causing £18,000 worth of damage to the property.

As the effects of the wine began to wear off, Kathryn did wonder how she had managed to cause so much destruction, but she never once felt any regret for her actions. She knew that if she had not done it then she would have continued seething about him for the rest of her life.

Next morning, Kathryn awoke, still in a partial drunken stupor. She heard the noise of someone smashing open the door that she had double-locked before collapsing in one of the spare bedrooms in the early hours. Kathryn realised it had to be the police and, for ten long seconds, considered climbing out of the window and making her escape. She knew that her life was about to undergo the most incredible, radical change but she felt strangely at peace with herself. Later, she compared it to the feeling of a condemned man on death row.

She stumbled out on to the landing to be greeted by two police officers. Graham Partridge was standing sheepishly behind them. She knew – they all knew. No explanation was necessary.

'I am not mad. I am not mad. I am not mad.' She repeated the words over and over again. Kathryn was well aware that she was guilty and would go to jail for what she had done but she had been perfectly content to wait for the cavalry to turn up and arrest her.

When she got to the police station a short time later, she even went through the charge sheet systematically ticking off the items she had destroyed. The police recalled her as being remarkably business-like about the entire incident.

.    .    .

At Swansea Crown Court, in January 1991, Kathryn pleaded guilty to a charge of criminal damage, and the following March she was sentenced. 'There were gasps in the court but I was expecting it,' she later recalled.

Kathryn was sentenced to six months in jail but was released after three months for good behaviour. Recorder David Hale said that she had been guilty of wanton destruction and had jeopardised her career as a lawyer. 'You have a volatile nature. What you did that night cannot be unpunished or overlooked. There is some truth in the psychiatrists' opinion that you derived some gratification from your notoriety. It shows your complete lack of remorse.'

Mr Tom Glanville-Jones, defending, had appealed to the Recorder to make a probation order so that Kathryn could continue her studies if allowed to do so by a disciplinary committee of the Law Society. 'This is a young woman who enjoyed a relationship with a much older man of some distinction. It was a relationship with no future. Mr Partridge must have known that, but he was prepared to be selfish about it.'

. . .

In January 1992, Kathryn was released from prison and resumed her career as a solicitor after telling reporters: 'I give a new meaning to the term criminal lawyer.'

Since her release she has moved back with her parents in Llangoedmor, in a house just a stone's throw from Graham Partridge's farmhouse. The former lovers do not even acknowledge each other in the street.

Kathryn said: 'I want nothing more to do with him. When there is a fundamental breach of trust in a relationship all respect is lost. I don't regret what I did.'

After her spell in prison, Kathryn said she wanted to work in the area of civil-liberties law and to champion prison reform.

'I've changed as a person. I've moved left of the spectrum.'

# 16

'Revenge, at first though sweet,
Bitter ere long back on itself recoils.'

*Milton, Paradise Lost* (1667)

# THE TOON CASE

Miguel Bravo was hard-working, mild and very overweight. He was shy, the sort of guy who would look at the floor when you talked to him. His wife Lucia matched him nearly pound for pound. She was not shy.

Lucia – who was sixteen years his senior – was considered an extremely possessive wife by most of thirty-eight-year-old Miguel's relatives. Many friends of the couple believed he was actually terrified of his strong-willed wife.

Miguel earned a lowly $16,000 from his job in a glass factory near the couple's home in Los Angeles and Lucia always insisted he should hand over his entire weekly wage packet. She rarely offered him any of his hard-earned money back, not even the price of a beer.

*Lucia Bravo, fifty-six, whom Californian police believed tried to kill her husband FIVE times before finally murdering him.*

After Miguel and Lucia married, his relatives warned him that the relationship was sure to end disastrously. They believed she was a bad woman who had an unhealthy influence on her husband.

By 1985, Lucia Bravo was also spending her husband's money on regular, unexplained visits out of Los Angeles. Miguel never once demanded an explanation from his wife; he just wasn't that kind of guy. If she needed to go away now and again then so be it. In any case, he was a bit scared to ask her because he knew she would get very angry with him.

The Bravo family had other mounting problems at that time. They were deeply in debt after investing heavily in buying a number of properties locally. By 1988, they faced a flurry of foreclosure notices and unpaid utility bills.

One night, after one too many arguments, Miguel surprised even himself with his courage in asking Lucia for a divorce. She was stunned. How dare he ask her for a divorce, she thought to herself. I will never allow it to happen.

However, Miguel was deadly serious. He had thought long and hard about it and come to the conclusion that Lucia would be better off without him. This wasn't a matter of a husband wanting to run away from his wife to marry some new, young floozie. Miguel genuinely believed he would be doing her a favour by splitting up.

Lucia definitely did not appreciate the finer reasons for her husband's request for a divorce. She looked at it in terms of pride and her Guatemalan background would never permit such a thing to happen. The fact that she was enjoying an extra-marital affair was irrelevant. Men in her home country did it all the time. Why shouldn't she have some fun?

However, Miguel was adamant. A few days after requesting the divorce he moved out of the family's modest single-storey home despite a dire warning from Lucia: 'You are shaming me. I will not let you divorce me, ever.'

Just a few weeks later, the house was raided by burglars who stole everything of value owned by the family. When Miguel popped round to pick up some clothes, he was shocked to find that many of his most prized possessions had gone.

Shortly after that, someone set fire to his car when it was parked outside the cheap motel where he was staying. The police were called but there were no witnesses. Unfortunately, Miguel was not insured.

Then, on 18 November 1988, as the day shift began at the glass factory where Miguel still worked, a white Ford Falcon made a U-turn and parked across the street. At five minutes before six, Miguel emerged and crossed the dimly-lit street. Suddenly, three shots rang out and Miguel crumpled to the ground. A bullet had lodged itself in his jaw and knocked out half of his front teeth. No one got a good look at his assailants or even managed to get the registration number of the car which sped away moments after the attack.

Three days later, Lucia Bravo, then aged fifty-two, visited the Los Angeles Police Department's Wilshire Division, which was then handling the case, to report that she suspected her husband's assailants were one of several moneylenders to whom she and Miguel owed money.

When police visited these moneylenders, they categorically denied all involvement and within three months of the attack on Miguel, the entire investigation had ground to an inactive halt.

Although Miguel eventually recovered from his injuries, doctors said the bullet would have to remain in his jaw for the rest of his life. Lucia was pleasantly surprised when Miguel announced that he was moving into an apartment near their home. She believed that she could still save the marriage, even though her illicit sex sessions with her secret lover continued.

A few days later Miguel narrowly escaped serious injury, or death, when someone else took a pot shot at him outside his new apartment. Three months after that came a third attempt on Miguel's life, when someone else blasted at him in the street, narrowly missing him and his car. Somebody clearly wanted Miguel dead.

A short time later, Miguel was bent over checking the oil level in his car when a fusillade of bullets zinged over his head, missing him by just a hair. A short while after that, a car tried to force him off a motorway while on a trip to Bakersfield, one hundred miles north of Los Angeles.

Miguel was genuinely, and perfectly understandably, fearful for his life by this stage. He knew that someone was out to kill him and he started to tell friends and family that he thought it was only a matter of time before they got him. Miguel began moving around the city, living sometimes with friends, sometimes even in his van.

When Miguel's sister Rosa suggested that Lucia might be behind the murder attempts, he refused to believe that his wife was capable of such a thing. Miguel was so determined not to believe what his sister was saying that he yelled at her: *'Tiene embrujado!'* (You are a witch!) He really believed that his sister was bewitched and determined to poison the good name of his estranged wife.

Then, on 24 September 1990, a pipe bomb exploded under Miguel's Thunderbird. Detectives called to the scene were intrigued because there are very few such attacks in terrorist-free Los Angeles. Detective Lawrence Garratt was particularly fascinated after he encountered the terrified Miguel Bravo, who miraculously survived the blast despite injuries to his buttocks and groin.

The case became known at the LAPD as the 'toon case' after the tough-to-kill cartoon characters. It was almost as if Miguel was as indestructible as Tom the cat. However, this was far from a laughing matter.

Detective Garratt found himself drawn to the case because so many aspects of it just did not add up. He knew instinctively that someone close to Miguel had to be behind the attacks. But what was the purpose of them? The Bravos had denied to Garratt that they had any insurance and he had no legitimate way of checking whether they were telling the truth.

Meanwhile, Miguel Bravo was becoming extremely depressed. He told his sister that he felt his days were definitely numbered. She urged him not to remain in Los Angeles, but Miguel's life revolved around the city and he felt it was his home. In June 1991, he visited his brother and made an offhand remark about planning to drive up to Bakersfield to pick up a car part.

On 26 June, a security guard found Miguel Bravo's body on a dusty piece of ground next to a cotton field canal, just off the old California 99 Highway. Miguel's wallet was still in his pocket, untouched. Kern County Sheriff's detective John Soliz was puzzled by the sobbing of Miguel's widow when he broke the news to her; *he could not see a single tear.*

Within hours of hearing of her husband's murder, Lucia Bravo was tactlessly suggesting to Miguel's relatives that they should purchase the cheapest coffin available for him. She even arrived late at the funeral when it was held a few days later in Central Los Angeles.

Five months later, an insurance investigator contacted Detective Garratt at the LAPD to verify that Miguel had been murdered, as his wife had just filed a massive insurance claim against his death. Then Garratt got another call about a policy Lucia had taken out, and another and another. In all, a total of five separate policies were taken out during a fifteen-month period before Miguel's death. They all listed Lucia as the main beneficiary.

Confronted by investigators, Lucia at first denied that she had even known of the insurance policies. Then she claimed that Miguel had insisted they keep them all secret. A grand jury subpoena of the Bravos' financial records showed that Lucia Bravo was inexplicably paying premium after premium even while banks were foreclosing on their properties.

Finally, after piecing together a paper trail that took more than two years to compile, authorities arrested Lucia Bravo in Arizona where her son said she had moved to escape threats from her late husband's relatives.

To this day, the authorities don't know for sure who pulled the trigger but prosecutors at her trial – which is expected to be held some time in 1995 – are planning to reveal that she collected a total of $700,000 worth of life-insurance policies. Lucia Bravo faces the death penalty if convicted of first-degree murder.

# 17

*'Blood cannot be washed out with blood.'*

**Persian proverb**

# OVER THE
# MOON

The freakishly hot weather in the middle of May 1992 was the final straw for Sarah Graham-Moon. She was feeling lonely and unwanted. Her two sons were now grown up and living away from home. Her only 'job' – if you could call it that – was hiring out herself and her eight gundogs to local shoots in the Berkshire countryside around her pretty home. Her husband had moved into a nearby property with his pretty, young, blonde mistress.

What really angered Sarah was that her husband, baronet Sir Peter Moon, always seemed to get precisely what he wanted. Even when they were together, he was the one who travelled round the world first-class, stayed in the best hotels, mixed with the jet-set, while she stayed at home with the children and the dogs.

To add fuel to the fire of her anger, Sir Peter had asked for a divorce eighteen months earlier and had then proceeded to behave as if the very mention of the word divorce was enough to give him a licence for romance.

To Sarah, however, the divorce would not be final until it had reached the absolute stage. She was perfectly happy to end their union in an amicable, civilised manner – until he decided to move into his mistress's £150,000 cottage in East Garston, just a short distance from the family home among the Berkshire horse-racing fraternity.

Up until that point Sarah had genuinely wanted the marriage to come to a peaceful ending. She had even hoped she could remain friends with Peter; after all, they had endured twenty-seven years of marriage. But it was not to be …

.  .  .  .  .

When the couple had moved to the house, they were already in the throes of divorcing but the property seemed large enough to allow them to live at opposite ends of it. The other reason for staying under one roof was to try to conduct their lives with some sort of dignity for the sake of their two sons Rupert, aged twenty-four, a student, and Thomas, twenty.

All Sarah ever wanted was a simple existence. Life in the village of Lambourn Woodlands tended to consist of horses and dogs, gumboots, dog baskets, dog leashes, an Aga in the kitchen and a grandfather clock in the hall, plus the obligatory sporting prints and drawings galore.

The grounds of the house were filled with Labradors in kennels and cats basked on the lawn among the poppies and roses. It should have been a perfect example of country living, but it wasn't.

Yet, when Sarah had first met Sir Peter in 1965, it had all seemed so different. She had been bowled over by his charm, wit and grace. He was a fun kind of man who bounced into a room and immediately caught everyone's attention. The Savile Row suits, the sports car, the hand-made shoes all seemed to add up to a very classy chap. She never questioned his choice of career as a second-hand-car dealer.

In those days, Sarah was known as 'Sally' to all her friends and family. The moment she agreed to marry Sir Peter, he insisted that she revert to 'Sarah' because 'Sally is a maid's name for goodness' sake,' he explained to his young bride-to-be.

Years later, Sarah looked back at that moment and realised she should have known then what she was letting herself in for.

.    .    .

In May 1992, when Peter announced that he was moving in with his mistress, it had come as a dreadful blow to Sarah. At fifty-four, she was no longer in the prime of youth, so to lose Peter to a trim-looking forty-year-old added to her hurt and anger. Sarah felt a kind of gnawing jealousy that would not stop growing. She looked on her husband's affair with Amanda Acheson as a typical example of a man in his midlife crisis finding a new love. It was all so clichéd. She was annoyed because other women seemed to behave so stupidly sometimes.

The full horror of what was happening gradually dawned on Sarah as her dreary life alone continued to go from bad to worse. She began to feel as if she was the one being punished.

Even more irritatingly, that other woman had insisted on calling her up a couple of times to explain the situation and offer her condolences for the end of the marriage. Sarah did not give a damn about Amanda and to have her trying to offer sympathy was doubly irritating. All Amanda could keep saying was that she had been through a similar situation.

Worse still was the fact that Sarah had to drive past the cottage her husband was sharing with Amanda virtually every day and she knew that the entire village was talking about the romantic upheavals with great relish. Sarah kept hearing things about Amanda. That she was tall and blonde and attractive. That she was a jolly, sporty type, and so on. However, one close friend did happily inform Sarah that her rival 'didn't need to wear a brassiere because she's a bit flat-chested'. Sarah knew her husband's tastes and she believed Amanda's lack of a bosom would deprive Sir Peter of one of his fondest pleasures in life.

During those long, lonely nights with only her dogs for company, Sarah certainly began to brood. She started to admit openly to herself that she was jealous. It was only natural that she should feel that way considering the length of her marriage to Peter, although she was adamant that there was no way she wanted him back. His decision openly to romance a woman who was living so close by was the final straw and it made Sarah feel so humiliated.

What irked Sarah the most was all that fun Peter had enjoyed. Throughout their marriage he had made new friends easily and had frequently gone to dinner parties without her. The ultimate insult was that since moving in with Amanda, he had shown up at all sorts of functions with her on his arm, including the local race courses. Sarah could only ever recall going to work functions with other second-hand-car dealers when she had been with Peter.

Sarah was feeling extremely cut off. Since moving to Berkshire after selling their house in Devizes, Wiltshire, three years earlier, she had found it difficult to make friends with the locals. They seemed rather snooty and uncommunicative.

However, what really niggled at Sarah was the fact that when they sold their earlier house for a vast profit of more than £300,000, she had bought their next home with some of that cash and her husband had received the other £150,000 and had not to her knowledge spent any of it on the home.

Sarah firmly believed that her seething rage would have been cooled by her close friends if she still lived in Devizes, but there was no one to turn to in Lambourn Woodlands. Her isolation was growing by the minute. She was so alone that sometimes she felt as if she could fall downstairs and no one would ever find her. She started to wonder if she was going crazy with the anger and frustration. Perhaps she was just becoming some kind of mad, middle-aged, menopausal woman. She started to realise that if she was to rid herself of this seething hatred she had to do something positive. She had to tell Peter in no uncertain terms how she felt.

She thought that perhaps the answer might lie in doing something really completely over the top. She wanted to make a point in the only language she believed he would understand, which was extremely infantile. For Sir Peter Graham-Moon was nothing if not childish. He might have been forty-nine years of age but he still retained a silly, schoolboyish sense of humour and Sarah reckoned she knew how best to deal with that.

Every time she stopped trying to think of a way to get revenge, other nagging feelings would enter her head. She started to get very frightened. She had always believed in the sanctity of marriage and she did not want to be left alone for the rest of her life. She was over fifty years of age and having to face a terrible truth – she was an unqualified, untrained, middle-aged woman. What future was there for her?

Yet here was a husband who had merrily informed her over the previous few years that he had fallen in love with women in all four corners of the world. The twenty-seven-year-old in South Africa was a classic example. One night he had proudly showed Sarah photos of her half-naked on a beach, as if seeking her approval in his choice of young mistresses.

Life seemed to be one long treat for Peter. He was doing things that Sarah would have loved to have done when they were actually married if only she'd been given the chance.

The way he had revealed to Sarah his affair with Amanda did not exactly help the situation. He had simply turned to her one day and said he had something to tell her. A few days later, Sarah heard he had been bragging about Amanda at the local pub.

She spoke to his mistress on the phone one morning when she called to ask him to come and see her to discuss some of the finer details of the divorce. Peter didn't bother going round to Sarah's until two hours later. That further infuriated her. How dare he treat her like some irritating aspect of his life. She was due some respect, surely?

While waiting for him to turn up that morning, Sarah decided it was time for action, time to show him that he could not continue to get away with humiliating her. She was suffering from an extraordinary version of sexual jealousy. She didn't want her husband in her bed but she didn't want him in anybody else's bed either.

That night, dressed only in her nightie and with a torch in her hand, Sarah smashed open the door to the cellar that held her husband's beloved collection of vintage wines. Minutes later she had loaded seventy bottles into milk crates and carried them up the stairs to her Volvo estate car parked in the driveway to their pretty home. She then drove six miles to East Garston and began a very unusual 'milk round'.

At 3 a.m., she arrived at her first port of call, the luxurious home of a millionaire. She was determined to make sure that every inhabitant in the village found a bottle of her husband's most treasured booze on their doorstep. Then she headed for the village war memorial. By the time she had finished, everyone had a few free bottles of vintage port and wine – some of it worth as much as three hundred pounds a bottle.

Next morning, to the horror of Sir Peter and his new mistress, seventy bottles of his favourite and most prized Chateau Latour and vintage port were sitting next to the milk bottles in the picturesque village of Lambourn Woodlands, Berkshire.

However, Sarah's revenge had not ended there.

After an exhausting morning walking the gundogs and cleaning out six chicken houses in the grounds of the house, Sarah decided it was time to slash the sleeves from Sir Peter's Savile Row suits, each of them worth a conservative one thousand pounds.

Then she headed for Peter's love nest where she put three bottles of his booze on top of his BMW before splashing five litres of white gloss paint all over the car. She then threw three of his suits on the bonnet, having cut four inches off each arm. She had been careful to cut off only one cuff because, as she later explained, 'men like him only use one hand'.

As Sarah dropped the remains of the last paint pot on to the bonnet of the car she began to realise just how easy it had all been. She also felt one hell of a buzz – a better feeling than any drug could provide.

The only slight disappointment was that she had forgotten to superglue a marzipan model of a hippopotamus to the bonnet of his car. The animal was a reminder of the days when Peter weighed twenty stone and his friends had nicknamed him Hippo. She had wanted him never to forget that fact. The only other thing she later wished she had done was to drop all his cigars in the horse trough.

She genuinely believed he deserved what he was getting. She knew what would hurt him the most and had delivered it with cunning precision. It never even occurred to her that it was wrong. This was something that she and thousands of women across the country must have wanted to do for years to their faithless husbands.

It was not Sarah's intention to draw attention to herself. She simply wanted to teach him a very public lesson about the most basic aspects of reasonable behaviour. The worm had turned and now Peter was paying a high price for all those years of misery he had inflicted upon her. She could have smashed all his bottles into tiny pieces but that would have been pure sacrilege. It was much more fun to leave a little trail of them around the entire village.

Sarah convinced herself that none of this was done out of spite. She just wanted to get his attention and make him realise how unhappy she felt about him flaunting his illicit relationship under her nose.

Throughout her attack and the distribution of the wine, she felt frightened yet elated at the same time. She knew she had to be brave enough to take him on and she knew he would realise why he deserved to be the recipient of such drastic action. After all, she was the one who was regularly kicked in the teeth. Amanda wasn't the only woman he had been to bed with since their marriage all those years earlier. Perhaps it wouldn't have been so bad if he had carried on that relationship away from her prying eye, but he didn't. It was almost as if he was getting some perverse delight out of cohabiting with another woman in front of her. Even then, when he conducted his other affairs in various parts of the country – or world for that matter – he still insisted on telling her all about his escapades. He had inflicted the first round of damage.

However, Amanda was the final insult. He had only to wait for a few more weeks and the decree absolute would have come through. But like some animal on heat, he could not hold on.

. . .

After the attack, Sarah stopped the entire divorce process until she got precisely what she wanted in terms of a settlement. As far as she was concerned, that 'bastard' had spent all her money and now she was exacting some revenge. She started to believe that all of his womanising was probably some sort of delayed reaction to the male menopause. She thought it significant that he had lost all that weight, making him even more vain than he had been before. It all began to add up.

Unwittingly, Sarah Moon had, in her own words, 'landed on a hornets' nest' when she achieved worldwide notoriety through her revenge-inspired attack on her husband's belongings. One crazy act had dispelled all her pent-up anger – and had the unexpected side effect of making her fleetingly famous.

She never, in a million years, imagined that her gesture would attract such attention. Surely, she thought, thousands of women respond to rejection this way. Yet the world's press now beat a path to her door. The last time her name had appeared in the papers was when she had won a potato-race at the local gymkhana. Within days of the news of her actions being reported in the British tabloid press, she found her life regularly punctuated by calls from America, Ireland, Australia, the whole world wanted to hear about the wife who got her own back in such magnificent style.

At the nearby stables where Sarah had deposited some vintage port, racehorse trainer Mark Bradstock and his lads drank a toast to Sarah's grand gesture. One of them said: 'I think Sarah has shown she has a pretty well-developed sense of humour.'

Sarah herself told the world: 'He deserved it. I have quite a fertile imagination and I know what hurts him and where his soft underbelly is – and that's his material possessions.'

She even decided to form a club for women who need to assert themselves and share experiences of being some-times down, but never out. She entitled it the Old Bag Club (OBC). Conditions of entry were that members were single and over forty.

'In the past I was an attractive woman. People would look at me when I walked into a room and I grew to expect that. As the marriage went on I didn't care one way or the other. Now that I have started to go out again, I notice that when I go into a room no one looks at me. But now I am discovering new things about myself.'

Sarah's moment of glory – however enjoyable for a gawping world, and however much she relished the applause – was ultimately fleeting. She seemed to the world the type of person who could cope with anything, but when Sir Peter appeared sheepishly at the house to collect his things and say a final goodbye, she felt a surge of anger returning.

'I hope I never see you again,' she told her husband.

· · ·

In October 1993, Sir Peter Graham-Moon married twenty-seven-year-old South African mother-of-four Terry de Vried. The marriage lasted just ten weeks.

# 18

'Is it not folly to punish your
neighbour by fire when
you live next door?'

Publilius Syrus, *Moral Sayings*
(first century BC)

# A FISTFUL
# OF DOLLARS

Cancun, Mexico, is one of those beachside paradises that most people can only dream about – miles and miles of pure white sand overlooking the Gulf of Mexico. A picturesque whitewashed town with a handful of luxurious hotels for wealthy American tourists, plus a scattering of bars and restaurants attractively decorated and designed to guarantee hundreds of thousands of visitors each year.

Mary Ellen Samuels from California had always wanted to go south of the border. It seemed so exotic on the television and it appeared to be the perfect place to escape from her worries back in California. So it was that attractive brunette Mary Ellen found herself on a get-away-from-it-all holiday. The perfect picture was made complete by the

*The cheeky snapshot of Mary Ellen Samuels lying in a sea of money just moments before making love with her secret boyfriend.*

presence of her young lover, who would provide the sex and cocaine that had been a staple need for Mary Ellen most of her adult life.

Most evenings, she and her lover would enjoy at least two bottles of wine in the hotel restaurant before slipping up to their suite where Mary Ellen knew that some athletic love making was sure to occur.

On one particular night they virtually had sex up against the bedroom door because their lust was proving so insatiable. Mary Ellen was always game to try anything within seconds of wrapping her arms around her young lover. For the first time in years, she felt completely free to do as she pleased. Her boring husband was dead. She no longer had to hide her secret vices from the world.

That evening she opened up a sachet of cocaine and laid out four, fat, two-inch lines of cocaine, then pulled out a handful of twenty-dollar bills before finding the crispest note which she expertly rolled into a makeshift straw before snorting her lines hungrily.

'I got an idea,' said her lover as he snorted the second of his lines. 'Gimme all the cash you got.'

Mary Ellen hesitated for a moment. She had worked and schemed very hard for her money.

'Come on. I ain't gonna take it. I just wanna show you how to have some fun.'

Then her handsome boyfriend started spreading twenty-dollar bills on top of the bed. Mary Ellen smiled and took a deep, excited breath. Earlier that holiday they had talked of making love in a sea of cash. Now their mutual fantasy was about to come true.

Mary Ellen stripped off her clothes and lay on top of the first layer of notes, then her boyfriend carefully covered her body with the rest of the crispest of the new twenty-dollar bills; their sharp corners enhancing the sensation of literally swimming in money. Mary Ellen could feel the notes cutting slightly into her nipples every time she moved while he continued to lay them all over her. It was a pleasant sensation.

Eventually, she was covered in the money, except for a small gap at the top of her thighs. He looked down at her face. It wore a smug, satisfied expression, then she slowly licked her lips with the tip of her tongue. Her young lover looked on in awe.

'Come on, baby. It's time to show me how much you love me,' exclaimed the sultry, dark-haired, one-time house-wife. She edged her legs apart a few inches. 'Come here.'

The woman dubbed by police as the 'Green Widow' was living up to her name. For her bizarre sex romp in a sea of money was just part of her celebration following an enormous insurance payout of half a million dollars after the apparently tragic murder of her Hollywood cameraman husband by a cold-blooded stranger.

A few months earlier, the slaying had struck fear into the suburban communities of the San Fernando Valley area of California, just twenty miles from the sprawling metropolis of Los Angeles. Inside the Hollywood movie community, many were mourning the loss of respected technician Bob Samuels, who had been closely associated with stars like Warren Beatty and Mel Gibson.

Sinking deeper into the mass of green paper, Mary Ellen pulled her young lover on to the bed and proceeded to make hot, passionate love. A luxurious life was, it seemed, sealed for ever.

With her neat hairstyle and fondness for sleek, well-fitting business suits, Mary Ellen Samuels certainly looked the part of a wealthy middle-aged widow, but she had been nursing a secret addiction to sex, drugs, drink and risk-taking for more years than anyone could care to remember.

It later transpired that this forty-five-year-old mother had ordered a hitman to kill her Hollywood cameraman husband – and then murdered the hired assassin once he had gunned down his victim. Soon afterwards she was dubbed the Green Widow after banking a fortune in insurance claims following her husband's death.

'It was a classic story of greed and manipulation combined with a callous disregard for human life,' said Van Nuys, California prosecuting attorney Jan Maurizi. 'This was a very attractive woman who had an uncanny ability to manipulate people and used her talents to get rich. Just about anybody whose life she touched became a victim. Basically, her husband was worth more to Mary Ellen dead than alive.'

. . .

This extraordinary story began on 8 December 1988, when Samuels's husband, forty-year-old Robert B. Samuels – who had worked on films like *Lethal Weapon* and *Heaven Can Wait* – was ambushed inside the house the couple had shared until their separation a year earlier.

The 'burglar' shot Samuels in the head with a 16-gauge shotgun. Police were alerted by Mary Ellen and her eighteen-year-old daughter Nicole after they arrived at the house to find her husband's bloodied corpse.

Samuels later boasted to friends: 'I should have won an Academy Award for my acting performance. I was the perfect grieving widow.'

However, detectives were suspicious because there was no apparent sign of a struggle. It also soon became clear that Mary Ellen was a very spoilt wife. She rapidly collected an insurance bonanza of $500,000 and went on a wild spending spree of parties, pals and drugs.

She splashed out $60,000 on a Porsche, rented stretch limos most weekends and even took her toyboy to Mexico to buy a villa in the sun. While on that secret holiday, she posed for photographs lying naked on $20,000 worth of the cash she had just been paid by insurers.

At the time of Samuels's death, detectives did not know that Mary Ellen's hitman, Robert B. Bernstein, had previously failed *three times* to knock off unsuspecting Bob Samuels.

Once Bernstein had plotted with Mary Ellen to push his car off a cliff and twice they had planned to shoot him after getting him drunk, but each scheme failed at the final hurdle. Finally, Bernstein had to hire another man – who later shot himself – to finish off Bob Samuels.

Explained prosecutor Maurizi: 'She was really pretty pampered by her husband. Her child was in private school. I think she had what the average American would consider the good life. But half of it wasn't going to be good enough for her.'

Also in court, Samuels's former husband Ronnie Lee Jamison conceded that she had been a compulsive liar who gambled and used drugs during their marriage.

Six months after Samuels's slaying, a botany professor on a nature hike found the body of suspected hitman Bernstein, a twenty-seven-year-old reputed cocaine dealer, which had been dumped in a remote canyon in nearby Ventura County.

It later emerged that Mary Ellen had hired two more hitmen to do away with Bernstein because he had started demanding more money and had threatened to go to the police if she did not pay. She paid her replacement hitmen a paltry $5,000 and a packet of drugs.

Stupidly, the merry widow insisted on keeping Bernstein's wallet in her Porche as a souvenir, where police later found it. They also discovered a diary for murder which read in part: 'People are saying I did it. Nailed me for Bob, want me for Jim.'

Mary Ellen's defence team even tried to claim that Bernstein – who carried a business card calling himself 'James R. Bernstein, specialist' – was smitten with the Samuelses daughter, Nicole. They insisted he acted on his own when he killed Robert Samuels after Nicole told him that Robert Samuels had raped her when she was just twelve years old.

Other friends and relatives of the couple insisted that Mary Ellen had arranged the killing of her husband in revenge for his sex attacks on her daughter. No one was ever able to establish if her claims were true.

Maurizi dismissed the sexual molestation charges as pure fabrication. Robert Samuels's sister, Susan Conroy, said: 'It's the ultimate betrayal. He isn't here to defend himself. Bob was a hard-working guy and he loved them very much. He would never have done anything to them.'

Paul Edwin Gaul and Darell Ray Edwards – the men who admitted killing original hitman Bernstein – testified against Mary Ellen Samuels after striking a deal with prosecutors who agreed to commute any death sentence against them. They were sentenced before her trial to fifteen years to life for the murder of Bernstein.

The Samuelses marriage originally broke up in 1987 when Mary Ellen moved out, taking the refrigerator and leaving a five-page 'Dear John' letter. She moved to a condominium in nearby Reseda, California. For more than a year, Mr Samuels hoped they might be reconciled.

However, reconciliation was far from Mrs Samuels's mind. One old family friend, Heidi Dougall, recalled: 'She hated him and she wanted him done.'

She even told friends that she had calculated that she would receive only $30,000 in a divorce settlement, as opposed to the $500,000 she knew her husband was worth dead.

Mary Ellen's biggest bone of contention with her

husband was over their shared ownership of a sandwich shop in nearby Sherman Oaks. She was also reluctant to wave goodbye to the $1,600 a month in maintenance that she was receiving.

During part of 1988, the vengeful wife once again told friends that she was considering having her husband 'done away with'. Soon she was even approaching her daughter's high-school friends. She insisted that she wanted revenge for her husband's attempts to molest her daughter. In one extraordinary incident, daughter Nicole even turned to a friend for help in the cafeteria. The stunned classmate later gave evidence against Samuels at her trial.

Even though Mary Ellen protested her innocence, the evidence was overwhelming and she was found guilty of two counts of murder, two counts of conspiracy to murder and two counts of solicitation for murder.

'I've never asked for the death penalty for a woman before,' said prosecutor Maurizi, who is still considering filing charges against Mary Ellen's daughter Nicole. 'But these murders were premeditated, six months apart and motivated purely through greed. Mary Ellen Samuels was a housewife who went shopping for something other suburban housewives don't need. She went shopping for killers!'

Maurizi also said to the jury: 'I ask you for a verdict of death for all the selfish and inhumane decisions she made in her life. I ask you, ladies and gentlemen, how many bodies does it take? We're talking about murder for the sake of the almighty dollar.'

On 16 September 1994, Mary Ellen Samuels became only the fifth woman in history to be sentenced to death in

California since the state reimposed capital punishment in the late 1970s. She will die in the gas chamber or through a lethal injection.

As juror Karen Hudson explained outside the court following sentencing: 'We wanted to let people know we were sure.'

# 19

'Heat not furnace for your foe so hot
That it do singe yourself.'

*Shakespeare, Henry VIII (1612–13)*

# DEATH ON A WATERBED

The shrill sound of a bell ringing loudly in the distance meant only one thing to Judy Benkowski – her husband was demanding something.

Clarence Benkowski was overweight and overbearing. All his life he had been number one in that miserable household. Even now, after retiring from his job as a welder, he expected to be waited upon hand and foot.

When his sick and aged mother decided to move in, things became even worse for Judy because it meant that now there were two of them bullying and cursing her; making her wait on them like a serf; treating her like dirt. There had to be a better life somewhere else, surely?

Often the two obese specimens would sit in the

*Three police photographs:*

Top left: *'Hitman' Eddie Brown.*

Middle left: *Judy Benkowski.*

Bottom left: *Debra Santana, Judy's neighbour and Eddie's girlfriend.*

Top right: *The house in Addison, Illinois, where Clarence Benkowski was shot.*

Middle right: *Det. Sgt. Tom Gorniak of Addison police, who immediately suspected Judy Benkowski of being involved in her husband's killing.*

Below: *Judy marries lover Clarence Jeske inside Dwight Correctional Institute, in Illinois, in August 1991.*

armchairs in the sitting room of their neat, detached suburban home at Number 508, South Yale Avenue, Addison, near Chicago, for hours on end without budging. That was when the little bell rang the most. An endless stream of demands followed.

*Ring:* 'Get me a coffee,' said one.

*Ring:* 'Get me a beer,' said the other.

*Ring:* 'This coffee's cold, get me another.'

*Ring:* 'This beer's not cold enough. Why haven't you kept them in the freezer?'

So it went on and on and on. Judy had no time for a job and only a small handful of friends in the entire world. Her only occupation was looking after those two leeches, as well as bringing up her two sons.

Not surprisingly, it often got too much for her. Her life was so relentless and so unenjoyable. She would cry herself to sleep at night, wondering when it would ever end. Occasionally, Clarence would drunkenly try to have sex with her. It certainly wasn't making love: in fact, it seemed more closely aligned to rape than anything else.

The act of sex was totally one-sided. He would make her fondle him and then – the moment he was ready – she would just lie there and listen to him grunting. Often she would try to think of other things, like the next day's shopping. Then he would hurt her with his roughness and that would snap her back to the unpleasant reality of having a huge fat lump of lard molesting her. The only good thing was that it was usually over in minutes, if not seconds. But there was so much pain involved. It was the sort of pain that inevitably occurs when an overweight old man forces himself on a slightly-built, five-foot-tall woman more than twenty years his junior. They might have been husband and wife in law but they were total strangers in every other sense of the word.

One day, however, Clarence decided he wanted to spice up his sex life, so he bought a waterbed. Typically, it was the cheapest one he could find and had the unpleasant side effect of being so overfilled that it made its occupants feel seasick.

The result was that Judy still lay there as usual every time he wanted sex – only now she had the horrible, over-whelming sensation of rocking up and down as if on a boat bobbing across the ocean.

It did help in one respect, however. Judy usually felt so nauseous within seconds of Clarence starting that he would often stop rather than risk being puked over.

Basically, Clarence's attitude towards sex was much the same as his outlook on life: men ruled the household, women were just there to honour and obey. He wasn't interested in Judy's feelings, he just wanted four big square meals a day and sex on demand.

For almost twenty years, Judy had put up with the insults and the appalling stress of married life. What else could she do? She had no career, no existence outside those four walls. She had been trapped for so long that she had forgotten what it was like to enjoy herself.

.   .   .

'You cannot let him treat you like this. You've got to do something about it, Judy.'

Debra Santana was outraged by her friend's complete acceptance of her distressing marital situation. She had heard so many horror stories from Judy. How could a husband treat his wife so badly? Debra assured her friend that she certainly would not put up with it.

Judy protested in her quiet, reserved way, 'What can I do? I have nowhere to go. No means of support.'

However, Debra was determined to help her friend and neighbour. Theirs was an unlikely friendship. Debra was a striking blonde aged thirty-two with a fun-loving attitude towards life, who had suffered during her marriage and taken the easy way out – divorce. She was enjoying everything that Judy had long since given up hope of ever seeing.

The main object of envy between the two women was Debra's athletic, black lover who gave her all-round satisfaction and never treated her badly. Judy was very jealous of Debra's lifestyle. She so wanted to feel warmth, passion and true love again. Judy knew Debra was right when she said she had to do something. But what?

Clarence, a strict Catholic, would not even discuss the subject of divorce. It wouldn't have been so bad if he had been prepared to let them lead separate lives. Then she could have gone out with other men and he could have done as he pleased. However, Clarence believed he owned Judy lock, stock and barrel. She was his woman. If he wanted instant sex, he should get it. If he wanted to insult her, he could. If he wanted her to be his slave, nothing could stop him, or so he told Judy with great relish.

Debra told Judy that there was no way she should accept this for the rest of her life. She might be thirteen years younger than Judy but Judy was finding herself increasingly influenced by her younger, more outrageous neighbour. The more they talked about Debra's adventures, the more Judy began to realise how desperate she was to end the misery.

'But what can I do about him?' Judy asked her friend one day.

'I've got an idea …' replied Debra.

·     ·     ·

Eddie Brown had given Debra all the sexual satisfaction she had ever craved. Even fully clothed, his muscular torso was literally bursting his shirt buttons. Judy Benkowski felt a tingle of excitement as she shook his hand for the first time. She imagined that Debra must have enjoyed some outrageous sex with this handsome stud. Only one thing about Eddie did surprise Judy: he was just five foot three inches tall. In fact, Debra towered over him by a good four inches.

'Not only is Eddie great in bed, but he's also going to help you with your problem, Judy,' chipped in Debra when all three met up.

Debra, Judy and Eddie had business to discuss because Debra had convinced Judy that Eddie was going to be the perfect man for a very special job for Judy. And it was a job that required a certain amount of planning.

'D'you really think you can kill him without being caught?' Judy had to confront him with the facts about the job at hand. He had told Debra he could murder Judy's husband with 'no trouble'. He had even agreed a fee of $5,000. However, they had to sort out details like where it should be done; what weapon should be used; how could they make sure the police did not suspect anything; what if he lived?

For a few moments, Judy wondered if she had gone completely crazy. How could she even contemplate murdering another human being? It all seemed like a dream. She hesitated. 'Maybe we should rethink all this.'

There was brief silence from her two accomplices.

'What?' said Debra. 'You can't change your mind. We agreed on this, Judy. Come on. Let's do it!'

Then Eddie chipped in, 'Yeah. It'll be easy. We can make it look like a burglary. No problem.'

The pressure was mounting on Judy. She wasn't a strong-willed woman at the best of times. She felt as if there was no choice in the matter. This was her only possible escape route from a miserable life. This was the one answer to all her problems and unhappiness. Certainly it seemed drastic, but then what more did that animal of a husband deserve? He had treated her like dirt for too long. Now it was her turn. Revenge would seem sweet. There was no turning back.

First there was the small matter of how and where to do it.

It was mid-October 1988, and Hallowe'en was fast approaching. Judy had a great idea, she told her two partners in crime. 'I'll get you [Eddie] a real scary costume. You're so short you'll look just like a kid out trick or treating. Then you'll knock on the door, Clarence will answer and you'll blast him away with a gun after saying "trick or treat".'

Debra and Eddie looked stunned. It was a preposterous

plan and they knew it but Judy seemed really attracted to the ghoulish aspects of it. She even laughed excitedly as she described the plot. 'He never likes to give anything to anyone who comes knocking at the door. I kinda like the idea of him getting the ultimate "trick".'

The earlier, hesitant Judy had been completely replaced by a hard-nosed would-be killer getting into the mood to murder. Her hunger for his death surprised even her two friends. She had now fully accepted the whole plan as a *fait accompli*. The risks involved were being outweighed by the fast approaching scenario – a new life without Clarence. Judy was feeling happier than she had done for years.

'But hang on there, Judy,' said Eddie. 'Trick or treaters don't tend to gun down their customers. The cops would know it was a contract hit straight off and they'd get us for sure.'

Eddie was trying desperately to defuse the situation. He had agreed to murder this woman's husband because the guy sounded like he deserved it, but the scheme Judy had just described was absolutely insane. It was like something out of a comic book, hardly the sort of low key-killing Eddie had in mind.

Judy was having none of it. She reckoned it was the perfect plan. 'The cops will think some crazy trick or treater is out there blasting innocent people to death. They'll never suss it as a contract killing.'

Debra and Eddie glanced at each other and shrugged their shoulders.

'You're the boss, lady,' said Eddie. Jobless and just out of jail, he needed the money, so he wasn't about to blow the contract, whatever the risks.

.  .  .

Hallowe'en trick or treating involves children dressed in spooky ghost or witch costumes knocking on the doors of houses in their street and shouting 'trick or treat' when someone comes to the door. Inevitably, a liberal helping of sweets is offered to the children and everyone goes home happy.

In the Chicago suburb of Addison, they tended to celebrate Hallowe'en just as fervently as in the rest of the United States, where the tradition first emerged thanks to the activities of a group of devil worshippers more than two hundred years ago.

South Yale Avenue – where the Benkowskis lived – was as traditional as it was typical: row upon row of three-bedroomed detached bungalows built to maximise the use of the space available. It was classic middle-American suburbia.

On the night of Hallowe'en that year, Eddie Brown began to wonder what he had got himself into. As Judy and Debra adjusted the ghoulish face mask they had bought for him at the local store, he felt that dressing up like a kid going out trick or treating contrasted rather disturbingly with his real mission as a professional killer seeking to murder a housewife's elderly husband.

To make matters worse, the latex mask was very uncomfortable. The two women had insisted on getting one that covered his entire face so that no one could see what colour his skin was. However, it was so airless behind that mask that Eddie was thinking he might never make it to number 508 alive! He was gasping for air before he'd even left the house.

'This is crazy. I can't even see properly out of the eye slits.'

Eddie's voice was so badly muffled by the mask that the two women did not even hear him at first.

So he yelled: 'I SAID THIS IS CRAZY.'

If Eddie was going to have to shout this loudly to be heard, then he'd probably alert the entire street when he went knocking on Clarence's door to announce his trick or treating campaign.

Eddie was about to walk out into the street when his face dropped. (Well, it would have if he had not had that latex mask on.) There were dozens of children wandering up and down the street in their trick or treating disguises. It was almost as if the entire population of under-fifteen-year-olds in Addison had decided to hit South Yale at exactly the same time.

Eddie ripped off the mask in a fit of fury and started to jump up and down on the spot in his white skeleton costume. The two women looked at him incredulously.

'I am not doing this. I can't start shooting at the guy in front of all those kids. I'll never get away with it.'

The entire plan had always had a ring of insanity about it. He decided to abandon it there and then before it was too late.

Judy was furious. She had hoped that she was just twenty-four hours away from never having to see that ugly hulk of a husband again. Now Eddie had ruined all her hopes and desires. 'But we have to do it, Eddie. You cut a deal.'

Judy was getting very angry but Eddie had no intention of not carrying out the killing. He just felt it needed a new plan. 'Don't get me wrong, Judy. I will kill him. But not tonight. It would be crazy and we'd all end up in jail.'

Judy reluctantly agreed with him. 'OK, but we gotta do it soon.'

. . . .

*Ring:* 'Where's my breakfast?'

*Ring:* 'Come on, I'm hungry.'

*Ring ... ring ... ring ...*

Clarence Benkowski was giving his usual pre-breakfast performance in precisely the same way he had done for the previous twenty years. His mother was visiting relatives so at least Judy didn't have to tolerate her. In the kitchen, Judy muttered quietly under her breath: 'Don't worry. You'll get just what you deserve in good time.'

If Clarence had not been so incredibly lazy, he might have got up from the breakfast table where he was slouched and lumbered into the kitchen to witness Judy pouring the contents of twenty sachets of sleeping pills into his coffee. Instead, he just kept on ringing. *Ring:* 'Move your ass woman. I'm hungry.'

Clarence was actually helping to sentence himself to death. Ringing that bloody bell yet again was the signal that marked the beginning of the end of his life, for it guaranteed that Judy felt no guilt as she emptied the contents of those packets and then swilled them around in his coffee. The more he rang the bell, the better she felt about killing him. It was a wonderful feeling just to contemplate the end of such an awful era in her life.

'Just keep ringing, Clarence. Just keep ringing. Soon you will never get another chance.'

AN EYE FOR AN EYE

Judy's only error was rather stupidly to tip the empty pill packets into the trash can before moving towards the dining area with a spring in her step, a bounce in her walk.

'There you go, sweetheart.'

She hadn't called him that for years. 'Sweetheart' was a term of endearment. How could she even contemplate feeling warmth towards the man she was about to have murdered? But Judy's passions were already rising at the very thought of his demise. She felt a tingle of excitement as she put the tray down on the breakfast table.

She sat at the table and sipped quietly at her tea but her eyes kept straining upwards and across the table towards Clarence. He hadn't got anywhere near that coffee yet.

Clarence was a predictable creature of habit. He liked to gulp down his fried eggs first and then stuff some toast in that big fat mouth of his. Judy knew that cup of coffee would soon be lifted to his lips. *'Be patient. Relax. He's going to drink it. All in good time. All in good time.'*

*The Chicago-Sun Times* was spread across the table in front of Clarence, as it always was each morning. Something caught his eye. He stopped eating and gasped at the sports results.

Not once had he ever made conversation with Judy over breakfast, or any other time for that matter. Clarence was not about to break the habit of a lifetime, but the cup of coffee remained untouched. Judy's initial burst of excitement was rapidly turning to desperation. *'Come on! Come on! Get on with it!'*

She was feeling desperate. It was time for desperate measures. 'Sweetheart,' for some weird reason she used that word again. 'Sweetheart, drink your coffee or it'll get cold.'

For a split second, Clarence looked at his wife quizzically. She *never* spoke at breakfast. Why the hell was she nagging him to drink his coffee? Never before in more than twenty years. Why now?

However, as with most things in Clarence's life, he gave it only a brief thought. Any further analysis would have been completely out of character.

Judy was annoyed with herself for weakening in the face of such adversity. What on earth was she doing trying to make him drink the coffee? It was a sure way to guarantee he'd get suspicious. She did not dare to look up again in case he caught her eye and saw the signs of guilt. He might even read the murderous intentions that filled her mind every moment as they sat at that fateful last breakfast.

Judy was getting very anxious. Maybe she had blown it? Perhaps he'd sussed her out? She shut her eyes for a split second in the hope that all that doubt and anguish would go away. Then it happened. The harsh slurping noise was like music to her ears. She opened her eyes once more to see that he was gulping it down at a furious rate, desperately trying to wash all that food down his big, ugly gullet. Now he was about to pay the ultimate price for his greed.

First one whole cup went down, then another in quick succession. Judy could feel the rush of relief running through her veins. She sighed quietly to herself. It was one of the most satisfying moments of her life.

. . . .

'I don't feel so good. I think I'll lie down a while.'

The sleeping pills were at last taking effect. Eddie had provided very precise instructions on how many she should feed him. Just enough to knock him into a deep slumber rather than complete unconsciousness. That way no one would be able to tell he had been drugged.

Just then Clarence got up and struggled towards the bedroom. He only just managed to reach that wretched waterbed before collapsing in a heap. Judy crept into the room after him, just to make sure he was out. Then she phoned Debra and told her, 'He's asleep. You better tell Eddie and get over here.'

Judy slammed down the phone and awaited her two accomplices.

Debra was the first to arrive at the house. She hugged Judy warmly in an effort to show her good friend that she supported her completely and utterly. The two women sat side by side on the sofa in the front room and counted the minutes until Eddie arrived. They soon heard the back door opening and then their hired killer walked in.

In an eerie silence, Judy handed Eddie her husband's World War Two Luger pistol and motioned him towards the master bedroom. They did not want to risk waking Clarence. Meanwhile, Debra put on a pair of stereo headphones and started listening to heavy rock music. It was a bizarre reaction. Maybe she was trying to blot out the noise of the gunfire that was about to occur?

The two women sat together on the sofa. Eddie had earlier said he would use a pillow to muffle the sound of the gun but Judy still heard the muffled pops of the three bullets being fired into her husband. It was nothing like what she had expected, but she showed no emotion. At last it was over.

However, there was still work to be done. Judy and her two friends had to make it look like a burglary that had gone wrong. The two women and Brown began tearing the house apart in convincing fashion. They pulled drawers of clothes out and spread them all over the bed where Clarence lay. Incredibly, the waterbed was still intact, despite the rain of bullets. Judy was disappointed in a way because she really did hate that waterbed. On the other hand it would have caused such a mess if it had leaked everywhere.

Meanwhile, Eddie was smashing the place to bits to make it look like a genuine burglary. Some of his blatant destruction was proving much more stressful to Judy than the murder of her husband.

'No. Not the china, please.'

Judy would not allow Eddie to destroy her vast collection of china. She had lovingly collected it over many years and it was the one of the few things in that house that she cared about. Eddie was incensed. 'But this is supposed to look like a burglary!'

'Just leave it. We can still make it look good without wrecking my china.'

Eddie just shrugged his shoulders. She was paying him so it was up to her.

A few minutes later, it was time for Eddie to make his escape out of the back door. First there was the matter of payment. Judy handed over one thousand dollars as his first instalment and also allowed Eddie to take two rings from a jewellery drawer. The rest of the cash would be given to him within a week. Seconds later Eddie was gone.

Debra could clearly see the relief on Judy's face. The two women embraced. They had done it. They had got rid of the animal. There was a big wide world out there waiting to be conquered. Judy was about to start her new life. However, before they could leave the ransacked house, they needed to make sure the coast was clear. First, Judy checked down the street. It was mid-morning. Husbands were at work; mothers were out shopping. Not a person in sight.

.    .    .

The Italian restaurant where Judy and Debra went to celebrate was so crowded that they were hardly noticed. The only unusual thing about them was that they ordered a bottle of very expensive white wine. As few people drink alcohol at lunchtime in middle America their toast to one another did not go completely unnoticed.

'To us. Long may we live without husbands.' The two women chuckled like naughty schoolgirls.

It wasn't just a new life of freedom that Judy was looking forward to; she believed Clarence's life insurance would be worth at least $100,000 and then there was the one $150,000 mortgage-paid house. Judy Benkowski was going to be a very merry widow indeed.

.    .    .

'He's been murdered. He's been murdered.'

Judy's screeching tones sounded truly horrific to

Addison cop, Detective Sergeant Tom Gorniak. He had been patched through to the Benkowski home after the nearby police station had received an emergency call from Debra and Judy, who had 'discovered' Clarence shot dead on their return from a 'shopping trip'.

In a bizarre, three-way conference call involving his patrol car, the police-station switchboard and Judy, Gorniak was trying to ascertain what had happened as he drove at high speed to South Yale Avenue.

By the time he rolled up at the house, an ambulance had already arrived. Gorniak immediately consoled the two women and got a uniformed officer to escort them from the property.

Then he began a detailed inspection of the premises. He knew he could not disturb anything until the crime-scene technicians arrived, but he was well aware that this was the best time to look around because everything was untouched and exactly as it had been at the time of the murder. He rapidly became puzzled by certain aspects of the crime.

The victim's body lay slumped in bed as if he had been taking an afternoon nap. How could he have slept through the noise of an intruder who then leant over him and fired three bullets into his head at close range?

Gorniak knew that few burglars would do that. In fact, even in trigger-happy America few burglars carry guns. A good burglar just gets the hell out of a house the moment he is disturbed. If someone stumbles upon him, his first response is to run – not shoot.

No, thought Gorniak, this victim was asleep when he was shot. He did not even have time to turn around and see who his killer was.

Then the policeman noticed the clothes thrown from the drawers over the body. That meant the killer had ransacked the room *after* the shooting. It just did not make sense. The intruder would have got out of there as fast as possible following the shooting.

Gorniak had been a policeman for ten years. He knew how dangerous it was to draw any conclusions at such an early stage in a murder inquiry, but he had no doubt that this looked like a contract killing.

.    .    .

'Did your husband have any enemies, Mrs Benkowski?'

Det. Sgt. Gorniak was trying to be as gentle as possible. After all, this was the apparently grieving widow he was talking to, and she appeared to be really badly cut up.

'No,' Judy replied. 'He had no enemies.'

Gorniak had a hunch. It was nothing more than that but it was enough to make him persuade Judy to stay on at the police station for a little longer that evening. He explained to her that he knew how awful she must be feeling but it really would be in everyone's interests if she stayed behind. Judy agreed. She did not want to appear to be hindering the police inquiries in any way.

Gorniak and his colleague Detective Mike Tierney began gently probing the widow for clues. They were convinced that there was still a lot more to tell about this case.

Judy, meanwhile, was getting edgy. She knew she had to tell them something. Maybe a half truth would solve her problems. Then they would leave her alone, surely? 'I did see someone outside the house this morning,' she recalled anxiously to the two detectives.

Gorniak and Tierney raised their eyebrows. Why didn't she mention this before? Judy then described in vivid detail how she had returned from her shopping trip with her friend and they had seen this rather short, stocky black man.

'He seemed to be running away from the house,' explained Judy.

The two officers were very surprised. They started to pull in the reins a little bit. They sensed that Judy knew more than she was revealing.

The next step was to haul Judy's friend Debra Santana in for questioning. As the detectives waited with Judy for her friend to arrive, they tried an old and trusted technique.

'It would help us if you could tell us everything you know,' said Gorniak.

Judy waited for a moment. She had a lot on her mind and those officers were well aware of it. 'I think I knew the black guy who was running from my house. His name is Eddie Brown. He is Debra's boyfriend.'

Tom Gorniak and Mike Tierney raised their eyebrows. They knew they were about to hear a full confession to murder.

· · ·

In September 1989, Judy Benkowski cried when she was sentenced to one hundred years in prison for hiring hitman Eddie Brown to murder her husband.

Du Page County prosecutor Michael Fleming had argued that Benkowski should receive the death penalty but

Judge Brian Telander ruled that there were mitigating factors that 'precluded the imposition of the death penalty'. These included no prior criminal record, numerous health problems and several character witnesses who testified on her behalf.

Fleming described the sentence – which means that Benkowski will not be eligible for parole until she is ninety-seven – as 'fair and appropriate. She claimed she wanted a divorce and he wouldn't go along, but she never even talked to a lawyer about it.'

.    .    .

On 31 August 1991, Benkowski married her sweetheart Clarence Jeske at the Dwight Correctional Institute in Illinois. The couple had first met before her husband was murdered but they both insist their relationship did not begin until after the killing.

By a strange twist of fate, Jeske now lives in that same house where Clarence was murdered in South Yale Avenue. He has even been made legal guardian of Judy's two children by her marriage to Benkowski.

# 20

'The infernal serpant; he it was,
whose guile
Stirred up with envy and
revenge, deceived
The mother of mankind.'

Milton, *Paradise Lost* (1667)

# FIFTH TIME
# LUCKY

As they kissed each other full on the lips, she pushed her tongue deep into his mouth. Then she felt his hands pulling and squeezing her breasts through the tight-fitting silk blouse she was wearing. His forefinger and thumb were expertly tweaking the firm, acorn-shaped nipples which peeped through the cream-coloured lace bra. The newly-weds were about to make the ultimate commitment on the first night of their marriage.

Then they fell back on to the vast king-size hotel bed and lay there locked in a passionate embrace. She was starting to relax with a man for the first time in her life. She had always promised herself that she would not make love until she had found the perfect partner. Now that dream was coming true – and it was proving to be just as amazing as she had hoped.

She stroked him gently. He winced slightly at first and she pulled her hand away momentarily. Then he guided her back almost immediately and smiled at her. It was a look of reassurance. He wanted her to continue her exploration.

Their hearts were throbbing in tune with each other. She stroked him and coaxed him once her hand had got used to the feel of the silky naked flesh. He moaned with pleasure. It was like music to her ears. For the first time in her life she was leading a man on and she adored the sensation of knowing that she could make him sigh with ecstasy at the very touch of her hand.

She knew it was the right time. After all, he was the man who had promised to honour her "til death us do part'. She could not wait to feel him making love to her, lovingly, knowingly, sensitively.

He had always seemed to enjoy every single moment of passion they shared, even when she denied him the opportunity to perform the ultimate act until they were married. Now she was giving him more pleasure than he had ever thought possible.

Sometimes in the past, he had sought out the services of local prostitutes because he felt frustrated by her refusal to make love. He convinced himself that he was doing her a favour by going with the street walkers because it stopped him from feeling the urge to ravage her, despite her protests.

Strangely, he found that paying for sex had been rather satisfying because it required no effort. He would often leave his wife-to-be at her parents' house, having achieved only a lingering kiss on the doorstep. Minutes later, he would be crawling the kerbs of the nearby red-light district looking for a suitable sex partner. Ironically, his beautiful bride's sex ban had driven him into the arms of dozens of other 'riskier' women. The strange thing was that he felt no guilt about having sex with the prostitutes. They provided a service which he was more than happy to take advantage of.

Most of the girls were gaudily dressed, humourless females who considered their job to be a form of self-inflicted torture that had to be endured because it helped to pay the rent and cover the cost of clothing their children.

However, there was one particular favourite who was not like the rest. She was at least forty years old with long, dark, flowing hair which successfully hid the giveaway lines which so often appear around the face and upper neck. He had found her attractive the first time he saw her and he tried desperately to find her each time he came looking for a woman.

It was not just her looks that he found so satisfying. She had an experienced eye. She had been a street walker for more than twenty years yet she spoke in a way that you would not expect from a lady of the night. She summed him up perfectly the first time they met. 'You don't get it at home, do you?'

He did not reply but his silence was confirmation of the facts.

She had a certain wisdom about her. She never made him feel dirty or guilty and she liked to talk and laugh. It was that sense of humour that set her apart from the rest.

There was also a hidden bonus. During the months that he went to her, she began to teach him things about sex that he never knew existed. In a weird way, it helped him to prepare for that first night with the girl he had just married.

. . .

The heat in the hotel bedroom was intense on that first night of their marriage. Outside it was around eighty-five degrees. Inside, it must have been close to one hundred. The sweat that covered both of their bodies made it seem even more exciting. He loved the way his hand slipped across her ample breasts. She adored the stickiness of his hairy thighs as she stroked him.

The more foreplay they engaged in the more she found her sense of enjoyment increasing. She had had no idea that making love would be as good as this. All the earlier tension and fear had long since subsided. In its place was a floating sensation. Just one spark would be enough to send her shuddering to a climax. But there was so much more to be done.

The sheets on the bed had long since slid off in the heat of their passion. Their slippery, sweating bodies were glistening in the neon light of the flashing hotel sign just outside their window.

She kept fighting the urge to have him inside her because she wanted to experience every other pleasure first. She ran her mouth down to his nipple and bit sharply. He smiled to himself for a moment; it was exactly what his favourite prostitute used to do on each occasion they had sex. Thinking about that other woman increased his pleasure even further.

He grabbed her wrist and tried to stop her but she carried on relentlessly, pushing and pulling. Then he grabbed her wrist really tight and she pulled her hand away in pain.

'That hurt.'

He did not reply but smiled back at her and began to make love. She felt a twinge of pain as he entered her and a tear rolled slowly down her cheek. She had an uncomfortable feeling about the agony he had just inflicted.

All the pleasure subsided from her body and she just lay there pretending to moan as he grunted into her neck. Her head was turned to one side and she looked out at that flashing sign through the window and wondered why he was making absolutely no effort to kiss her on the lips.

. . . .

The first few months of marriage were fairly uneventful for Jean-Louis and Patricia Orionno. He worked hard in the day at his job in the bank and she kept their flat in the pretty French town of Doubs immaculately clean for when he got home each evening.

Patricia did not really know what to expect from marriage. She often used to think back to that first night of their honeymoon and wonder if she had somewhat over-reacted to his one small sign of brutality towards her. She worried about it because, ever since that incident, she had never come anywhere near an orgasm during relentless nights of torrid sex with Jean-Louis.

She had tried to talk to her mother about it one morning when she was at her house but the only information she could gather from her mother was a deep-set distrust of men in general; in the eyes of her mother most men were lusty animals who expected sex whenever and wherever they wanted it. Women were the victims who simply had to open their legs and obey their master's every command.

Patricia was shocked by her mother's opinion. It made married life sound so depressing. Why on earth hadn't she told her daughter all this before she walked up the aisle?

'Well. You have to get married, don't you?'

It was, as the French say, a *fait accompli*. However, that was not good enough for Patricia. She wanted more than just a servant–master relationship from her marriage. She also wanted to learn how to enjoy sex rather than feeling as if she were being hit by a battering ram each time he forced himself upon her.

The main problem was that Jean-Louis was more interested in his own satisfaction. Certainly, he had tried to excite her in various ways but she always felt as if he was just going through the motions. It was as if he felt obliged to make her feel a little excited before the actual act of sex. As all women know, however, there is a lot more to passion than just a token gesture of foreplay.

One night, Patricia tried to stop Jean-Louis from just jumping on top of her and he got very angry. 'Why are you stopping me? I have a right. You are my wife.' In those words lay the root of all her problems. He considered sex as something his wife should never refuse. If she did not want it then she was expected just to lie there and pretend to enjoy it so that he could get his own dose of satisfaction.

Poor Patricia had not even had the pleasure of a full,

uninhibited orgasm. She was fed up with reading about all the wonders of sex in women's magazines. She wanted to enjoy it for herself.

They appeared such an attractive couple and seemed so much in love but beneath that veneer of happiness lay a frustration with life so deep that it was tearing Patricia apart. To make matters even worse, she had no one to tell about her problems. Instead, she bottled up the anger and bitterness. It was a vicious circle. She rapidly lost all the vitality and charm which had made her so attractive to Jean-Louis in the first place. In their stead was a seething bitterness with the role she was playing in his life.

Jean-Louis worked so hard at his job at the local bank that he did not even notice his wife's change of attitude. He was happy just as long as he ate good food, drank good wine and enjoyed lustful sex.

His idea of a dream evening was to walk in from work, smother his wife with kisses, lift up her skirt and make love to her on the kitchen table. That would be followed by a wonderful four-course meal washed down with a subtle claret and maybe a cognac to round things off. Then he would retire to the bedroom where he would blow garlic-encrusted fumes all over his attractive wife's body as he crushed her under the full weight of his passion.

Unfortunately, Patricia got more satisfaction out of seeing him enjoying her cooking than through any of his demands in the bedroom. And things were going to get worse and worse ...

.  .  .

As the months of marriage turned into years, the couple's inability to produce any offspring seemed to increase Jean-Louis's sexual appetite. It was as if he was trying to prove his masculinity by forcing himself on her every single night. However, it was not just a ten-minute grope in bed that he was expecting. As he stepped up his demands for more sex, he did what many husbands do and began trying to make his wife 'experiment'.

As a rule, both parties have to be in complete agreement if the question of unusual sexual practices arises. Experts say that you can do what you like within the four walls of your own home just as long as both partners are prepared to explore new boundaries.

Patricia was not even consulted by her husband when he decided she should be handcuffed to their four-poster bed and whipped. He just forced her down on the mattress one night and – gripping her wrists just as he did on their honeymoon – he spread her arms and her legs wide apart and attached the cuffs to the bedposts. She began to wonder how many times he had done this to other women.

As she lay face down on the bed, she was thankful for only one thing; she did not have to see his drunken, glazed eyes feasting on her as he whipped and abused her body. Patricia's sexual unhappiness had turned into real torture which would ultimately prove too much of a burden to tolerate.

If Patricia had had someone to pour out her feelings to, then the mounting anger and bitterness might not have reached such a dangerous climax. She was living on the edge. Each time he came near her she shuddered but she had to let him do whatever he wanted to because she was afraid of being punished really severely or even worse, losing the home she had spent so much time and energy creating.

What hurt her most was the emotional torture of knowing that her own husband did not care how much he abused her body. His idea of sexual satisfaction seemed to be to damage her body and force her to degrade herself by performing sick, perverted acts too unpleasant to publish in any detail here.

Patricia's daytime hours were like a temporary escape from the monster who ruled her life with a rod of iron. She would often cry for hours and hours at the kitchen table each morning. Eventually, however, those tears were replaced by a new determination. She could not take much more of it. It would soon be her turn to make him suffer.

. . .

Patricia crushed the white sleeping tablets and mixed them into the meat pie. She wanted to make sure there was absolutely no sign of them when he devoured the dish on his return from work that evening. She reckoned that twenty pills would probably be enough but she added a further ten just for good measure.

As Patricia stirred the thick stew of meat and gravy, she felt a surge of happiness for the first time in months. He had driven her to these desperate measures. The previous night he had left her tied to the bed for hours while he whipped her and then performed the most dreadful sexual act she had ever experienced in her entire life. When he was finished doing that, he insisted on what he considered to be perfectly normal love making, but the love had long since disappeared for Patricia; it was just adding to her misery. He did it for hours and hours. Eventually, she cried herself to sleep, in so much pain that she wondered how she would even be able to get up the next morning.

However, Jean-Louis had the answer to that problem. As the early-morning sunlight poured through the bedroom window, he pushed and prodded her until she woke and then performed yet more sex. The pain barriers had long since been bypassed by a numbing feeling that comes when you just don't care any more.

Back in the kitchen on that cold winter's night in early 1988, Patricia could feel the pain each time she moved. It was a constant reminder of the suffering he had caused her. It had also persuaded her to murder him.

Jean-Louis arrived home an hour later and all but ignored her. His only concern was to pull the cork on a bottle of his favourite red wine and start drinking. Patricia was delighted that her husband was being as uncaring as ever. She didn't want any doubts about her plans to kill him and she knew that if he showed her any caring attention then she might feel a twinge of guilt.

As her bullying, perverted husband tucked into his meat pie, he looked like a man without a care in the world. No doubt he was contemplating more sick sex later that evening. He was already treating Patricia worse than the prostitute who had taught him so much all those years ago.

Patricia watched him consume every mouthful of the pie with great relish. He was so selfish that he did not even bother to ask why she was not joining him for supper. He did not care just as long as she gave him what he wanted.

Ten minutes later, Patricia saw her husband finish the last scrap on his plate. He even greedily wiped it clean with a piece of bread. She was so happy. It would not be long now, surely?

Jean-Louis was a fairly well-built sort of fellow, more solid than rotund. He had a typical Frenchman's cast-iron stomach, used to devouring all sorts of gastric oddities, but Patricia's poisonous pie was certainly managing to have an effect.

He sat down on the sofa in their living room and let out a huge yawn. 'I'm feeling really tired. Shall we go to bed early tonight?'

Normally, that was the signal for the start of a round of sexual torture too painful to contemplate. This time, her husband's request met with a genuine response. 'What a good idea. You look shattered.'

Patricia was ecstatic. It was working. He would be unconscious in minutes. And there was an added bonus – she would not have to have sex with him that night either.

She was right. Jean-Louis was snoring away within a few moments of his head hitting the pillow. For the first time in years, Patricia Orionno sat up in bed and read a book. It was a romantic novel and it gradually reignited her hopes for the future.

She looked over at her husband snoring noisily next to her. '*Come on, die. Come on, die.*' But Jean-Louis looked rather too healthy to be anywhere near his deathbed quite yet.

It was a good book but Patricia could not concentrate. She kept looking over to see if he was dead yet. His snoring proved he most certainly was not. She was furious. *He had to be dead. He should be dead*, but he was very much alive. Even in his slumber, his face had a huge, broad grin on it as if he were challenging her to try to kill him.

Patricia had every intention of rising to that challenge. She got up out of the bed and crept towards the kitchen. Her fists were clenched in fury. She pulled open a drawer and took out the sharpest knife she could find.

She walked back into the bedroom, and looked down at his irritatingly content face and narrowed her eyes in determination at the task at hand. Then she stopped in her tracks. Should she just stab him over and over or slit his wrists gently and quietly without even disturbing him? With any luck he would be sufficiently knocked out by the sleeping pills not to feel a thing, whereas the force and violence required to stab him might awaken him. She decided to slit his wrists.

Like a mastercraftsman carving a small wooden figure, she began sawing at the veins on the back of his wrists. The knife seemed only able to penetrate the tiny blue rivulets that ran up his arm. She found herself desperately squeezing his wrists just as he had done to her on that honeymoon night. It was the only thing she could do to try to pump those veins up large enough to slice through them. The wounds she finally managed to inflict were pathetic. Little globules of blood trickled from the minuscule gashes, but there was no cascade as she had expected. Patricia did not realise that the massive dose of sleeping pills had slowed down Jean-Louis's circulation so much that, even if she had shot him in the chest at point-blank range, he would have been highly unlikely to bleed to death.

After ten minutes she gave up that method of killing. There had to be a better way. Or perhaps she should just give up altogether. It was actually starting to seem more appealing just to divorce the brute. Then she remembered all the appalling sex acts he had forced her to do and realised that she had to continue her mission.

Patricia then thought that the kitchen gas might do the trick. She ran the unusually long cooker hose pipe from the kitchen into the bedroom and pointed it straight into the snoring face of her husband. He did not budge an inch.

As the smell of the gas started to make her feel queasy and faint, she realised that she was in danger of killing herself in the process of trying to end her husband's life. She quickly abandoned the hose pipe.

There had to be an easier way. She stepped back from the bed for a moment and looked down at him sleeping peacefully as if he did not have a care in the world. He had no right to survive this onslaught but somehow he was still very much alive, if not exactly kicking.

Each time her murderous intentions failed, she felt a surge of even more fury and bitterness. She kept reminding herself of that abuse. She could still feel the pain he had inflicted on her. He could not be allowed to get away with it.

She reached down, picked up a pillow and held it up above her head. His face was looking up at her, challenging her to do it. She hated every inch of him. Even as he lay there in front of her, she could not bring herself to feel an ounce of sympathy for him.

Slowly and deliberately, she knelt over his chest. The

pillow was still held up high above her head. She crashed it down over his face and held it there with all her strength. She could feel him struggling beneath her. His arms came up and grabbed her breasts and then moved, blindly, up to her neck. He was hurting her now and her grip on that pillow was weakening. She could not hold it down tight enough.

He was starting to begin to take control again. Wide awake from his pill-induced slumber, he was fighting back and she was just not strong enough to stop him. She looked over at the knife with which she had tried to slit his wrists a few minutes earlier. It was her only chance.

She managed to lean over to the bedside table and grab it from the slippery glass surface. For a split second she fumbled with it as his right hand began hitting back at her to try to stop her. His face was still covered by the pillow but she knew that in another few seconds he would emerge victorious yet again unless she took her chance immediately.

She plunged the razor-sharp knife right into his chest and felt the blade slice through the skin and tissue like carbon paper. She had to be quick. This was her only chance. She knew that one wound would not be enough. She had to puncture his body until there were enough outlets to drain the energy – and the blood – from him.

Seven more times she slashed the knife into his torso. Each time she felt his body twitch in pain. It was a pleasant enough sensation after all the agony he had inflicted on her. However, he still refused to die so she just carried on stabbing into his body.

By the time she pulled the knife out for the eighth time,

she knew that he was finally dead. His body lay limp beneath her, the pillow still covering half of his face. However, she could see from the one glassy eye now staring out into oblivion that she had finally achieved what she had set out to do.

She felt nothing inside. Her conscience was not even troubling her. She got calmly off his body and gave him one last glance just to make sure there were no signs of life. For the first time in years she was free from the man who had turned her life into a living hell.

.   .   .

On 23 October 1988, Patricia Orionno was allowed to walk free from a court in her home town of Doubs, France, after the judge found her not guilty of the murder of her husband Jean-Louis.

He called her actions 'justifiable' following years of sexual torment at the hands of her lust-hungry husband.

# APPENDIX

'There are minds so impatient of
inferiority that their gratitude is
a species of revenge, and they
return benefits, not because
recompense is a pleasure, but
because obligation is no pain.'

Samuel Johnson, *The Rambler* (1751)

# FURTHER CASES

These days, life does indeed prove stranger than fiction. In addition to the twenty cases already described in vivid detail in *An Eye For An Eye* check out some of these examples to jog your memory about what happens when women get their own ideas about revenge.

## *Name*: Sandra Wignall, aged forty-eight

*Crime*: Arranged the murder of her husband as he fed foxes in a wood. Nine days after marrying Robert Wignall, Sandra plotted to kill Robert and cash in his life-insurance policy.

Sandra lured him to the woods and distracted him with a promise of sex while her ex-convict lover Terence and a second man pounced on him and stabbed Robert twice in the heart. (1990).

*Name*: Jean Daddow, aged fifty-three

---

*Crime*: Paid £12,000 to have her husband gunned down on their doorstep. Standing to inherit £300,000 from her husband, Jean plotted with a hitman and her twenty-three-year-old son from a former marriage to have him murdered. After he was gunned down, Jean ordered a gravestone saying 'Terence Daddow – taken suddenly. In God's house but in my heart, your wife Jean.' All three were found guilty of conspiracy to murder. (1991).

*Name*: Karen Randel, aged twenty-one

---

*Crime*: Karen, from Swansea, had been married to nineteen-year-old David Randel for just five months when he went out clubbing with a friend and bumped into a group of women from work. Karen, six months pregnant, was goaded by the women when she arrived at the club later. They hinted that they'd heard that she and David were getting a divorce. When Karen arrived back home, she plunged a

*David Randel, nineteen, was stabbed with a kitchen knife by his wife,
Karen, only two months after their marriage.*

kitchen knife into David's stomach, severed an artery and
he died. Karen was found guilty of murder but is appealing.
(1992).

## *Name*: Carmela Larmarque, aged forty-three

*Crime*: Paid out $20,000 to a hitman to have her husband
murdered. She pleaded guilty at her trial but the judge was so
sympathetic that he allowed her to be released after just six
weeks in a New Orleans psychiatric hospital. (1993).

*Name*: Elizabeth Litchfield, aged fifty-six

---

*Crime*: Plotted to kill her business partner in Norfolk by hiring a hitman to whom she promised a share of the £200,000 life assurance on the intended victim. Found guilty and jailed for seven years. (1994).

*Name*: Victoria Carr, aged eighteen

---

*Crime*: After her thirty-three-year-old live-in boyfriend dropped her and returned to his former lover, Victoria caused more than £3,000 worth of damage to their home in Honiton, Devon. Victoria splashed blue gloss paint on the carpets and furniture and scrawled messages on the the walls. She was conditionally discharged for a year, bound over to keep the peace for a year and ordered to pay £45 in costs. (1994).

*Name*: Christine Clark, aged forty-nine

---

*Crime*: Smashed her policeman husband's brand-new car with a hammer, causing almost £3,000 worth of damage, when she discovered he had been having an affair with a younger woman. Christine, from Leeds, admitted wilful damage and was conditionally discharged for twelve months. No order was made for the damage. (1994).

## *Name*: Angela Brooks, aged thirty-seven

---

*Crime*: Deliberately drove into her estranged husband's car after discovering he had been on holiday in America with his new girlfriend instead of paying maintenance for their three children. Angela, from Portsmouth, admitted two charges of criminal damage and was given a two-year conditional discharge. (1994).

## *Name*: Dee Knight, aged thirty-six

---

*Offence*: Filled fifteen paddling pools with repulsive food and laid them around the family house after her husband dumped her following just thirteen months of marriage. (1994).

## *Name*: Alice McNeill, aged thirty-five

---

*Crime*: Sawed her lover's bed in half and then went on a £9,000 wrecking spree after learning that he had cheated on her with a string of other women. Alice, from Staining, in Lancashire, was jailed for six months after admitting causing the damage, but her sentence was later overturned because of the circumstances surrounding the case. (1991).

*Names*: Charlene Maw, aged twenty-one, and
Annette Maw, aged eighteen

---

*Crime*: Killed their bullying father after putting up with years of torture and abuse at the family home in Yorkshire. The sisters were each jailed for three years after admitting the manslaughter of Thomas Maw. (1980).

*Name*: Marianne Bachmeier, aged thirty

---

*Crime*: Shot dead a man who had molested her daughter as he stood trial in court in Germany. Marianne, from the town of Lubeck, was sentenced to six years in prison after being found guilty of murdering Klaus Grabowski. (1983).

*Name*: Pamela Sainsbury, aged thirty-two

---

*Crime*: Killed her bullying husband Paul after enduring endless brutality at his hands. Pamela, from the west of England, was placed on two years' probation after admitting the manslaughter. (1991).

## *Name*: Te Rangimaria Ngarimu, aged twenty-eight

_____

*Crime*: The first woman contract killer to be brought to justice in Britain. She gunned down hospital patient Graeme Woodhatch because she was infatuated with a man who wanted Woodhatch killed. Ngarimu was jailed for life at the Old Bailey. (1994).

## MEL – THE INSIDE STORY
Mel Gibson is Hollywood's number one superstar. Yet there is a dark side to this extraordinary man. This devastating book strips bare the real Mel Gibson to reveal stories of girls, booze, drugs, brawls and much, much more.

## TOM CRUISE – UNAUTHORISED
This is the first definitive biography of Hollywood's most powerful star. *Tom Cruise – Unauthorised* is packed with new revelations about this most complex and enigmatic man. We learn of his deep involvement in the controversial Church of Scientology and of the outspoken political beliefs that hide a secret and astounding ambition. Of his poverty and his hurtling rise to superstardom. The author spent two years travelling the world, talking to those who know Tom Cruise best, to discover the real truth about this extra-ordinary man.

All prices include post and packing in the UK. Overseas and Eire add £1.00 to the price of each book.

To order by credit card, telephone 0171 381 0666.

Alternatively, fill in the coupon below and send it with your cheque or postal order made payable to Blake Publishing Limited, and send it to:

Blake Publishing Limited
Cash Sales Department
3 Bramber Court, 2 Bramber Road, London W14 9PB

Please send me a copy of each of the titles ticked below:

- [ ] Hell Hath No Fury — £4.99
- [ ] Like a Woman Scorned — £4.99
- [ ] Love You To Death, Darling — £4.99
- [ ] Doctors of Death — £4.99
- [ ] Mel – The Inside Story — £14.99
- [ ] Tom Cruise – Unauthorised — £14.99

Name .........................................................................................

Address ....................................................................................

........................... ........................... Postcode ...........................

Please allow 21 days for delivery.